Alissa
Tucke

At the thought, heat blazed through her body, a raging, unwise, uncaring inferno. Then she realized he was only nodding. When Tucker stepped back, she'd felt like they'd just ended an embrace, though they hadn't touched. "I'm going." She spun blindly and nearly tripped over her own feet and she'd hurried to her car, painfully aware of her own thoughts and painfully certain he'd read them on her face.

She fumbled for her keys and unlocked her car, only then noticing a single sheet of paper trapped beneath the wiper blade. The block-lettered words took a moment to register.

YOU'RE GETTING WARMER

She heard a click and then a detonation. And then the night erupted in searing, choking flames....

RICOCHET

JESSICA ANDERSEN

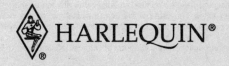

HARLEQUIN®

TORONTO • NEW YORK • LONDON
AMSTERDAM • PARIS • SYDNEY • HAMBURG
STOCKHOLM • ATHENS • TOKYO • MILAN • MADRID
PRAGUE • WARSAW • BUDAPEST • AUCKLAND

ISBN 0-373-22893-7

RICOCHET

Copyright © 2006 by Jessica S. Andersen

ABOUT THE AUTHOR

Though she's tried out professions ranging from cleaning sea lion cages to cloning glaucoma genes, from patent law to training horses, Jessica is happiest when she's combining all these interests with her first love: writing romances. These days she's delighted to be writing full-time on a farm in rural Connecticut that she shares with a small menagerie and a hero named Brian. She hopes you'll visit her at www.JessicaAndersen.com for information on upcoming books, contests and to say hi!

Books by Jessica Andersen

CAST OF CHARACTERS

Alissa Wyatt—Bear Claw City's new crime-scene artist wants to put down roots, but instead attracts the attention of a sinister serial kidnapper.

Tucker McDermott—In trying to protect Alissa from escalating danger, the footloose detective winds up with a partner...and a whole lot more. Will the growing attraction be enough to keep him in town? More important, will they both live long enough to find out?

Johnny Ferguson—The serial rapist vowed revenge when Alissa helped capture and convict him years earlier. Now he's out and looking for payback.

Cassie Dumont and Maya Cooper—Alissa's two best friends and coworkers in the forensics department want to keep her safe and catch the kidnapper, but interdepartmental politics may endanger them all.

Detectives Piedmont and Mendoza—The partners don't trust Alissa or her friends. How far will they go to prove that Bear Claw doesn't need a new forensics department?

Bradford Croft—The unassuming man lives next door to the first kidnap victim. He was previously convicted of a sex offense, but the evidence doesn't seem to directly link him to the kidnappings.

Michael Swopes—With a rap sheet and a suspicious purchase, Swopes seems like a strong suspect. But where is he?

William Parry—The chief of the Bear Claw police department will do anything to weld his officers into a team and find the Canyon Kidnapper.

Prologue

The collector unlocked the door with fingers that trembled, not from the cold but from excitement. He eased the shed open and let the cold winter sun splash across the soiled floorboards, let it touch the girl's bare, chilled foot.

She stirred and her dusky-blond eyelashes fluttered as though she still fought the drugs that swam in her bloodstream.

His lips curved into a smile and he whispered, "Perfect." She was perfect. Young and scared and too weak to run away, just the way he liked them. "She's perfect."

But you can't keep her, a voice said nearby, or maybe inside his head. *Stick to the plan.*

The collector scowled. "I don't want to. I'm going to keep her. She's mine. I picked her out. I took her. I can keep her."

No you can't. Stick to the plan—or else.

It wasn't the tone of anger—whether real or

imagined—that changed the collector's mind. It was the slice of fear that slipped into his chest, colder than the Colorado winter, reminding him of what would happen if he disobeyed.

"Okay, fine. Never mind. I'll do it." He opened the shed door wider and shook out the blanket he'd carried from his van. He leaned over and wrapped the girl, not to keep her warm, but to cover her from view, just in case. Then he lifted her off the dirty floor and carried her out into the light. He felt the snow crunch beneath his boots, heard the others calling to him from their sheds, and smiled.

Everything was going according to plan.

Chapter One

Alissa Wyatt pulled her VW into the back parking lot of the Bear Claw Creek Police Department—BCCPD—five minutes after the task force meeting was set to begin.

Damn. She hated being late. She yanked off her BCCPD ball cap, twisted her honey-colored hair into a businesslike bun and shoved her sketches into a nylon portfolio. Then she bolted for the back entrance, trying not to slip on a patch of ice and rock salt.

The fierce Colorado mountain winter was cold and raw, but to Alissa, it felt like coming home. Granted, *home* was a relative term in her experience, but that was the goal here, to make a home. To find a place for herself.

She shouldered through the heavy door and sped past the desk clerk, heading for the back conference room at a fast walk. Though Chief Parry might overlook her tardiness, the others wouldn't. Bear Claw Creek's finest had been slow to welcome the three women who made up the new Forensics Division. Not because of their sex, but because Alissa and her two best friends from way back in the Denver Police Academy had been brought in to replace Fitzroy O'Malley.

The now-retired Fitz was an icon. A one-man crime lab who'd been a fixture in the mountain cop shop since long before most of the veterans had been rooks. And now those rooks-turned-veterans resented the three-woman team that had been brought in to run the newly expanded Bear Claw Creek Crime Lab.

Worried about the impression she might make, Alissa broke into a jog while she shrugged out of her bulky parka.

"You're late," a voice said from behind her. The dark, masculine tones grated along her nerve endings, sending up sparks where sparks had no place being.

She froze midstep, set her teeth and turned. Everyone knew Detective Tucker McDermott could move as silently as a wolf when he chose to, but it was still unnerving.

Rumor had it he could hunt as well as a wolf, that he never gave up until he caught his quarry—at which point he moved on to another territory. Another hunt.

Typical, she thought with a twist of irritation that had very little to do with the man in front of her and every-thing to do with men in general. But fair or not, McDer-mott bugged her for a variety of reasons, not the least of which was his sheer presence. A hint of wildness clung to him as he stood opposite her in the hallway, making her think of mountain air and a hawk's cry, even when he was dressed for work.

The professionally starched, cream-colored oxford didn't mute the iron strength that shone in his six-foot frame, in the taut muscles of his shoulders and chest, and in the wide-palmed hands that held a pair of fat folders. Though he wore trendy slacks and polished leather boots, the city veneer didn't sink beneath his skin. His dark, wavy hair was too long for convention, his skin too burnished for a desk job, even in the depths of winter. And his eyes were the gleaming brown of Bear Claw Canyon at sunset.

Alissa's artistic soul took a snapshot, saving the image of wilderness contained within walls, even as her instincts for self-preservation sent her back a step at the look of pure masculine irritation in his eyes.

She forced a smile and cursed the churn in her stomach. "Glad to see I'm not the only one running late."

"Actually, you are. Most of us have been here since last night." He lifted the folders. "The chief sent me for rental records."

Alissa hid the wince and clicked her teeth together to stem the explanation. He didn't need to know that she'd logged over thirty hours in the past two days, talking with the victims' families and the witnesses—such as they were—trying to assemble photographs and sketches. Trying to get a sense of the crimes. What bound them together. What set them apart.

Patterns and the lack thereof.

What was the use in explaining? She turned away from him. "We should get inside."

She noted that he didn't open the door for her, and cursed herself for noticing. But before she could slip inside the packed-full room, he leaned down, close enough that she could feel his warmth and smell the woodsy scent that clung to him like a second skin.

"Don't worry, I won't hold the door for you. I remember that you don't like it."

The memory of that one stupid night, the temptation of it whispered along the side of her throat like a caress.

Yeah, she remembered, too. And, damn, she wished she didn't. That had *almost* been a colossal mistake. So she shot him a glare and hissed, "There's nothing to remember."

But as she stalked into the room and ignored the other cops' stares, his soft, mocking chuckle followed her. Shamed her.

Inflamed her.

Then she saw the photographs of three teenage girls tacked along one wall of the conference room, and Tucker McDermott, that night, and even her problems with her co-workers faded into the background as she was reminded why she was there. Why they were all there.

Three girls were missing, and their time was running out.

If it hadn't already.

Chief Parry stood at the front of the room, a fit, stern man in his late fifties, with salt-shot brown hair and a neatly trimmed beard. He didn't comment on Alissa's tardiness, but a roomful of eyes followed her to the single empty seat in the corner between Maya Cooper and Cassie Dumont, her friends and the core of the new Bear Claw Creek Forensics Division—BCCFD.

They sat as a unit, separated from the others.

Alissa tucked her portfolio between her feet while Chief Parry gestured toward the board, where the girls' faces were blown up larger than life. He touched the photo on the far left, which showed a fey-looking blond wisp of a girl with blue eyes and a gap between her front teeth.

"Three girls in three weeks," he said, voice somber. "Twenty-two days ago, sixteen-year-old Elizabeth Walsh was supposed to meet her friends outside the MovieMogul 10. She never showed." He moved to the middle picture, which showed a slightly chubby brunette wearing dark-rimmed glasses perched over a sprinkling of freckles across the bridge of her wide nose. "Four days later, seventeen-year-old Maria Blackhorse failed to meet her date at the Natural History Museum. Her parents didn't call it in for nearly forty-eight hours." He moved to the picture on the far right, which showed another blonde, this one model-gorgeous in her expensively posed photograph. "Then, two days ago, eighteen-year-old Holly Barrett disappeared sometime between noon and 4:00 p.m." He turned and scanned the room. "Three girls in three weeks, people. We haven't found their bodies, but we haven't found them alive, either. And I'll bet my badge that their time is running out."

Alissa didn't need Maya's psychology degree or Cassie's genius with chemicals and blood spatter to tell her that. She'd spoken to the two witnesses who thought they'd seen Elizabeth get into a light-colored van. She'd been to the victims' houses, talked to their parents.

And, yeah, she had a feeling they were running out of time, too. The longer a kidnapper kept his victims, the better his chances of discovery. Unfortunately, the criminals knew that as well as the cops did and had brutal ways of protecting themselves.

Chief Parry continued, "I want a quick report from each division, and then Agent Trouper will give us a rundown of what's going on at his end." The ten-day-old task force contained specialists and detectives from the relevant BCCPD divisions, including Homicide, Missing Persons and Forensics, plus Garrett Trouper, their FBI liaison. Parry nodded toward the corner where the three women sat. "Wyatt, you can get us started with Forensics."

Great. Just great.

Alissa set her teeth, lifted the portfolio, climbed to her feet and faced the room. She was thirty-one years old and an eight-year veteran of two different city police forces. She could do this.

But she was aware of McDermott leaning against the wall at the back of the room, alone. Aware of the other officers' eyes on her, men and women both, all wishing Fitz was there instead of her.

They weren't going to like what she had to report. *I've got nothing,* she wanted to say, *no reliable witnesses, no good sketch, no ideas. Nothing.*

Instead, she opened the folder, drew out the pitiful list of the suspect's possible physical traits and a sad description of the van, and handed it to a surly looking uniform in the front row. "Please pass these out for me." She addressed the group. "As you can see here, the two witnesses at the MovieMogul 10 were only partially helpful. They saw a man and a light-colored van, but couldn't be certain of either description…"

She continued to speak, but her attention was drawn to a stir of motion at the back of the room. When she looked up, McDermott was gone.

And a frisson of wariness told her something was up.

THE DESK OFFICER'S SUMMONS had pulled Tucker out of an important meeting, but he couldn't manage to be annoyed by the interruption. He'd been glad to escape the conference room. It was too hot. Too crowded.

Hell, who was he kidding? Any room with Alissa Wyatt in it was too hot and crowded for him. She was a hot ticket, a bundle of energy with the legs of a Vegas showgirl and the light-blue eyes of an artist. Half the men on the BCCPD were panting after her, and the other half wanted her gone.

Tucker straddled the two camps. He wanted her gone, but he didn't want it to matter. And it wouldn't have mattered if it hadn't been for that night, when he'd met her on a crowded dance floor and heard his favorite words, *I'm just in town for a few days.*

He wasn't proud of it, but vacation flings were his stock in trade. He was too much of a nomad for anything more, and at thirty-five was too damn set in his ways to change now. Hell, the one time he'd tried to settle down had been a disaster. He'd hurt a good woman, someone he'd cared about, though he obviously hadn't cared enough. Since then, he'd stayed carefully away from nesters, from women who wanted more from him than he was able to give.

So he'd danced with the just-in-town-for-a-few-days babe who'd introduced herself as Alissa. He'd reveled in the drape of her long, honey-colored hair as they danced close, then closer still. He'd slid his hands beneath her midriff shirt, riding on the high from closing the Vanzetti case, one too many beers and the gleam of encouragement in her eyes.

They'd kissed on the dance floor, then again in the hall by the phones, moving fast even for him. But the roar of heat had swept away rationality and battered at the small kernel of self-preservation he held close to his soul. They'd stumbled to her rental car wrapped in each other, not sure where they were going but positive they needed to get there quickly, before they proved that spontaneous combustion wasn't a myth.

Unable to wait for his place or her hotel, he'd pulled her across his lap in the passenger seat. She'd gone willingly, twining around him with arms and tongue until a flaming, pulsing need consumed him—nearly panicked him. It was too much, too soon, but the spark of caution was quickly gone. He fumbled for his wallet, for a condom, and knocked a badge off the center console.

Only it hadn't been his badge. It had been hers. And it had landed on a real estate printout of a cute house not five miles away from his generic apartment building.

Oh, hell, he remembered thinking when the explanation followed.

She was in town for a few days, all right. But she'd be back soon, and working for the BCCPD. His bosses. He'd excused himself without an explanation and bolted, unnerved by an almost overwhelming desire to stay.

Two weeks later she and her friends had replaced Fitz as part of Chief Parry's updating of the BCCPD, and she'd been under his skin ever since.

Because the knowledge made him mean, Tucker scowled at the male desk officer, a twenty-something named Pendelton. "This better be good."

Pendelton gestured at the chest-high counter, which held a plain paper rectangle with "Det. Tucker McDermott" printed in square letters with black ink. "I thought you should see this. It didn't come in the mail. It just sort of…appeared. One minute it wasn't there, and the next…" Pendelton snapped his fingers. "There it was on the front desk." A hint of nerves worked into his voice when he said, "I'm sorry. I went to the can for a minute. Just a minute, I swear. Maybe the dispatchers saw something." But he didn't sound hopeful.

Tucker's gut tightened. "Did you touch it?"

"No. Not on your life."

It could be a hoax, but instinct told him otherwise. "You got a pair of tweezers and a couple of evidence bags?"

Pendelton trotted off to get the items. For a brief second Tucker thought about calling one of the new evidence techs. Hell, they were just down the hall. He would have if it had been Fitz. But because Fitz had retired—very abruptly—and because Tucker knew the procedure as well as anyone, he took the tweezers himself. Teased the envelope open himself. And read the enclosed note himself.

Dumb cops. Elizabeth is in the canyon, and you'd better hurry. It's getting cold.

Adrenaline fired through Tucker's bloodstream. He bolted to the conference room and yanked open the door. The pretty, dark-haired psych expert of the new Forensics Department—he was pretty sure her name was Maya—stood at the front of the room with a string of words listed on the wipe board behind her, things like *white male, 20-40 years,* and *high functioning,* followed by a question mark.

Things they didn't need an abnormal psychology specialist to tell them. They were cops, damn it. They knew the profiles, knew what they should be looking for. They just hadn't been able to find the bastard yet. They'd needed a break.

Well, maybe they'd just gotten one.

Not caring that he was interrupting, Tucker lifted the note inside its protective evidence bag, blood racing with the thrill of the hunt. "Come on. The first victim is in the canyon."

Or else the kidnapper wanted them to think she was.

BEAR CLAW CANYON was shallower and narrower than some of the nearby natural wonders, but it had its own dangers, its own treacheries. The crevice was only man height in spots, but the waterway at the bottom meandered and doubled back on itself, breaking off into tributaries and feeder streams without warning.

Because of it, there were thousands of tiny, cracked caverns and overhangs, a hundred places for hikers to lose themselves in the two-thousand-acre Bear Claw State Park.

A hundred places to hide a girl. A body.

Near the snowy spot where they'd parked their official four-wheel-drive vehicles, Alissa curled her hands into fists and fought the urge to run for the canyon, to scream the missing girl's name. There were procedures to follow, and experience had taught her that protocol beat instinct every time in police work. A gut feel might lead to the perpetrator, but judges and lawyers cared about procedure. Words like *intuition* could get an important case thrown out, a violent criminal released.

The memory of just such a case soured the back of her throat.

Before the task force headed into the canyon, Chief Parry divided them into pairs. With the way Alissa's luck had been running, she wasn't surprised when the chief paired her with McDermott.

The detective didn't argue. He merely scowled and jerked his head toward their search area, a multi-branched point where the waterway widened and slowed. "Come on." He dropped down into the canyon, which was nine or ten feet deep, where their search was to begin. When Alissa paused at the edge, he frowned. "You want me to catch you?"

She shook her head. "No." *Hell, no.* "Just give me a minute. I want to get a feel for the scene."

Though skeletal analysis and reconstruction was her specialty, her official title in the BCCFD was Crime Scene Analyst. Captain Parry was counting on her to see, and record, the details others missed.

Sometimes the smallest detail could make or break a collar. A conviction.

She stood on an open expanse of rocky ground, half a mile from the main entrance to Bear Claw State Park. They had driven in, but parked well back from the lip of the canyon, which was maybe forty feet across at this point.

She saw no other tire tracks in the week-old snow. No footprints beyond those of the searchers. "He would have needed an ATV to get in here, a snowmobile or a four-wheeler," she said to herself. "Unless he carried her in."

If the girl was even in the canyon. The note could just as easily be an ugly prank.

Alissa let her eyes drop lower, to the crumbling canyon edge and the bare, frozen dirt nearby, where the wind had swept the area clean and drifted snow beside the ice-strewn waterway. It was a pretty scene, a coldly brutal one that reminded her of the frigid power of a mountain winter. But it told her very little about the crime or the perpetrator.

Satisfied, she sat at the edge of the canyon and

ignored McDermott's offered hand to drop lightly to the frozen ground below.

"Fitz took pictures," he said, voice dark with challenge. "Photographs are reliable evidence. Sketches aren't. Memories aren't."

"You think I don't know that?" She pulled her gloves out of her pockets and shoved her hands into them, though it didn't lessen the chill. She was tired of the BCCPD's attitude, annoyed by the closed-mindedness of the other cops. *Fitz did it this way.* "I'm not Fitz, but I'm damn good at my job. Don't lecture me."

"I'm not," he fired back, eyes dark with temper, and maybe something else. "It's just…" He blew out a breath. "Hell, I don't know what it is."

Except he did. They both did. The memory of that night at the dance club shimmered between them like a living reminder of passion. Of heat.

She slanted him a look and decided to tackle it head-on. "This doesn't need to be a thing, you know. We danced. No big deal."

Except that was a lie. It had almost been a very big deal for her.

She'd gone to the club that night with Maya and Cassie. The girls had been split up by their assignments after the academy, and though they'd kept in touch with calls and visits in the six years since, it hadn't been the same. They'd often talked about working together, so when they heard rumors of Fitz O'Malley's unexpected retirement, they'd put in a proposal and three transfer requests. A month later it was official. They were the new BCCFD.

They had met in Bear Claw that weekend to look at apartments, and had gone out for a celebratory drink after. One drink had turned into three over a couple of hours, along with food. Not enough to get Alissa blitzed, but enough that when the music started, she was right in the mix, bumping and grinding along with the dancers while Cassie and Maya cheered from their table.

Alissa had noticed the man's eyes first, dark and intense as he'd stood at the edge of the crowd. He wore casual jeans and an open-necked shirt, covering a tight, honed body that spoke of strength and the outdoors. She saw him shake off an invitation from a shaggy-haired blonde and another from a slick brunette, but his eyes never left hers. When she crooked a finger, he'd met her halfway.

As they had danced, she reminded herself she didn't do bar pickups. Hell, she hadn't done much of anything in the past year, since her supposedly serious boyfriend had taken a job out of state. He'd buggered off with barely a goodbye, making him no better than her father, who'd at least pretended he was going to keep in touch.

"It's not about what did—or didn't—happen that night," McDermott said, interrupting old, sour memories that deserved interrupting. "My only concern is finding these girls and catching the bastard who's taken them. I have nothing against you except that I work alone. I don't want a partner, so stay behind me and let me do my job."

He strode off without waiting for an answer, leaving

her to fume, as old and new irritations battered her heart.

"Let him do his job," she muttered, still standing where they'd dropped down into the canyon. "Great. Another cowboy. Maybe he'll get the guy, but the guy won't stay gotten, will he? He'll walk, just like Ferguson did."

At her last posting, a serial rapist had been preying on college girls, and the Tecumseh Springs PD had formed a task force similar to the one she was in now. They'd gotten the guy—a punk named Johnny Ferguson, who lived with his mother and hated the world—but there had been a glitch in the chain of evidence, a cowboy moment when the lead cop had gone on instinct rather than procedure and blown the case to hell.

Since then, she had valued precision over gut feel, evidence over emotion. It was an odd contradiction—an artist who didn't venture outside the box—but it worked for her. And that was yet another reason she should stay far away from Tucker McDermott, who had the reputation of being all about instinct, sometimes at the expense of procedure.

Knowing it, she steeled herself to follow him down the canyon, toward the sound of other searchers' voices calling for the missing girl.

Lizzy...Li-zzzy. The cries overlapped in mournful echoes, making the canyon seem alive. Making it seem as though something—or someone—was out there. Waiting. Watching.

Alissa held back a shiver, knowing that it wasn't even certain the girl was nearby. The note could be nothing more than a hoax.

Or a trap.

The feeling of watching eyes intensified, and Alissa scrambled to catch up. As though sensing the same scrutiny, McDermott glanced back over his shoulder. "Hurry up, *partner.*"

She ignored his tone and quickened her step—

And she saw it.

She couldn't have said why the crevice caught her attention, but something about it seemed off. Some might call it instinct, but she preferred to think of it as a highly developed sense of color and shape. Something was wrong with this picture.

She stopped dead and stared at a shadowy, snow-shrouded cleft in the canyon wall. Her mind took a snapshot of the scene. Then she did one better. She pulled out her slick camera and took a few shots, carefully overlapping them so she could reassemble the panorama later on her computer.

"You see something?" McDermott asked, but his voice seemed distant as she walked toward the cleft, her every instinct on alert.

It was a tunnel of sorts, an ice-and-snow overhang undercut by the trickle of a sluggish tributary that had long since frozen over. Totally focused on the scene, on her job, she snapped several pictures, then drew a small flashlight from her pocket. She crouched down and shone the light into the forbidding darkness.

At the furthest reaches of the yellow illumination, she saw a bare, motionless foot and the ragged hem of wrinkled blue jeans.

Excitement slapped through her, mixed with apprehension that the foot wasn't moving. "I see her!"

Alissa heard Tucker shout something, but she couldn't wait for him. Her heart thundered in her chest. If Lizzie was alive, every second could be vital. That was the protocol—administer necessary aid first, then protect the crime scene.

Nearly shaking with anticipation, Alissa pulled off her gloves and shucked off her bulky parka so she could fit into the narrow tunnel without disturbing evidence. She jammed the small flashlight in her mouth to leave her hands free and dove in headfirst.

Tucker shouted, "Wyatt, wait!"

"I'm fine," she called back, her flashlight-muffled words bouncing back from the ice and snow. "I've almost got her!"

Blood pumping, she crawled forward, careful to avoid a line of scuffs and boot prints preserved in the blown snow near the edge of the tunnel. Almost there! The girl's bare ankle looked more gray than flesh toned, except where raw places stood out in bloody slashes. She was curled on her side facing away from the tunnel entrance. She wasn't moving.

Alissa said a quick prayer, reached out and touched the motionless ankle. She felt the faintest hint of warmth. The flutter of a pulse.

"She's alive!" she shouted. "Get the MedVac helicopter down! I'm going to pull her out. When you see my feet, give a yank!" She reached forward and felt for the girl's other foot. There was something tied to it, maybe a length of the rope she'd been bound with.

Alissa yanked on the twine.

A bright white light flashed. An earsplitting crack reverberated through her skull.

And the tunnel collapsed on top of her.

Chapter Two

Ice, snow and dirt landed atop Alissa, pressing her down, squeezing the breath out of her. She screamed and tried to scramble back, but her arms and legs were pinned. Panic clawed at her throat, and her heart hammered in her ears. The weight increased, as though the whole canyon had come down on top of her.

She thrashed, squirmed and cried out with what was left of her breath. "Help! Help me!"

The tiny flashlight fell from her mouth, illuminating a small air pocket that had formed around her head. She saw dirt and ice six inches from her on all sides. Saw it shift a little closer as the cave-in settled.

"Help!" she whispered when she ran out of breath to scream. Cold, salty tears streamed down her face and ran into her mouth, and all she could hear was the pounding of her heart.

Calm down, she told herself. She had to calm down. *Think!* She tried to count her breaths, but she couldn't breathe, so instead she counted her heartbeat, which was too loud, too fast.

McDermott had been right behind her. He would get her out.

But what if he can't? asked a scared little voice in her soul. *What if he's too late?*

The panic crested again, and she moaned, wishing she could be anywhere else. Out with the girls for a round of Friday-night drinks. Visiting her mother, even. They weren't really close anymore, hadn't been since Alissa's father had left and her mother's middle name had become Bitter. In that moment Alissa wished she could see her mother now and say she was sorry for having been a snotty teenager and a distant adult. Sorry for having blamed her mother because her father had never come back for that promised visit. And in a crazy way, she was sorry she'd never searched for him, if only to tell him that he was a rotten jerk.

Her tears dried to cool wet tracks on her cheeks. The air inside the small pocket warmed and grew stale. She thought she heard a shout and dull thuds, but they were too far away. And she was all alone.

"You're going to be okay," she said aloud, her voice strengthening as the debris allowed her an inch of breathing room. "They're going to get you out of here."

She felt a hint of movement beneath her outstretched hand. Not shifting soil this time, but living flesh. Then she remembered. *She was holding the girl's ankle!*

"Elizabeth? Lizzie, is that you?" she called, not knowing whether her voice would carry far enough, but devastatingly grateful that the girl was alive. "If you can hear me, wiggle your foot a little."

The foot moved.

"Okay. Hold on for me, okay? They're going to get us out of here." Alissa bit her lower lip and forced her voice to be even. "I want you to stay calm and relaxed, okay? I'm a police officer, and my friends are digging us out right now."

She'd meant Cassie and Maya, who had been on the search team farther up the canyon and who must be frantic with worry. But her brain fixed on a picture of McDermott. She pictured him digging down toward her, eyes as dark as they'd been when the two of them danced.

Incredibly, the image brought a measure of calm.

Alissa drew a shallow breath to keep talking, more for her own sake than the girl's, but her words were cut off by a roaring shift of dirt. A far-away shout of panic.

The air pocket collapsed. Icy cold weight bore down on her.

And she couldn't breathe at all.

FASTER. HE HAD TO DIG faster, spurred by the knowledge that it had been a damn trap all along. The anger of it burned through Tucker's gut as exertion flamed in his muscles. He got his fingers around a chunk of rock and frozen soil and heaved it aside.

He cursed as he worked, cursed Alissa for not waiting for backup, cursed himself for not being close enough to stop her. Cursed the bastard who'd left a note with his name on it, then ambushed an officer.

A female officer.

Her sex shouldn't have mattered, but it did. Or maybe it wasn't just that she was a woman. Maybe it was this particular woman. Ever since that night at the bar, she'd been at the edges of his mind, tempting him to forget his own rules.

"It's settling!" shouted a tall blond woman he recognized as one of Alissa's friends. Cassie something. The other searchers had all converged on the spot, drawn by the small, deadly explosion and Tucker's bellow of shock and rage.

"We've got to get them out of there." Chief Parry scraped at the snow and dirt with gloved hands. "There can't be much air!"

Alissa's image flooded Tucker's mind, all honey-colored hair and warm blue eyes. Her remembered taste lingered on his tongue, though he'd told himself to forget it.

With a nearly feral roar, he lifted an ice-crusted boulder and heaved it aside.

"There!" Cassie yelled. "There she is!" She darted toward a scrap of cloth and a laced boot. "Get down here and help me!"

The others surged forward, but Tucker elbowed them aside. "I've got her!" He dropped into the hole and touched the limp body of the woman he was supposed to have been backing up. Who was supposed to have been backing him up.

This was why he didn't work with a partner. He was no good at teamwork.

He whispered a prayer, or maybe a threat, as he

checked her over and found nothing obviously wrong. She was stirring when he lifted her up and out of the hole. His muscles strained, though she couldn't weigh much more than 110, 120 pounds. He looked down and realized her hand was caught on something. He saw a flash of denim and shouted, "There's the girl!"

His shout brought a flurry of activity, of renewed digging, but Tucker focused on the woman in his arms. She moaned as he hauled her up and out of the ragged hole and carried her to the side of the canyon, where he could lay her flat as the BCCPD helicopter landed nearby.

She didn't stay down long. Within moments she was batting at his hands and struggling to sit up. But her attention wasn't focused on the rescued girl, whose motionless body was being strapped to a backboard for loading into the chopper.

No, Alissa was staring at the place where the kidnapper's bomb had blown away part of the tributary canyon wall.

"Look!" She pointed to the scarred rock and dirt.

He saw it then, and let out a soft curse at the object that had tumbled from the disturbed earth.

It was a human skull.

ALISSA WAS COLD and sore and scared, but she'd think about it later, when she was alone and nobody could see her lose it.

She'd been buried alive. She deserved some hysterics, but she'd learned to put off the tears long enough to deal with the immediate problem. When she was younger and her mother had been struggling to keep them together, the problem had usually been money—an irate landlord or a cold Denver apartment in January.

Now the immediate problem was a crime scene. Actually, it was two crime scenes, one on top of the other.

Who did the skeleton belong to? How had the person died? How had it come to be buried there? And what were the chances that the rigged explosion would accidentally open another, far older grave?

Very slim, which suggested they had been meant to find the grave. But why?

McDermott touched her arm. "They've got Lizzie loaded on the chopper. They're waiting for you."

"I'm fine," she said automatically, though her lungs ached at the words. She moved away from his touch, uncomfortable with how her chilled body yearned to lean into his warmth. She glanced at him and saw that his eyes were as dark as she had remembered, only with irritation, not passion. "Thanks for pulling me out."

She would never admit that thinking of him had kept her sane in those last few minutes. She'd used him as a mental crutch, that was all. A focus.

Instead of accepting her thanks, he snapped, "I wouldn't have needed to if you'd waited for me. What were you thinking? *Never* leave your partner like that."

Irritation sparked. "If you'll remember, *you* left *me* behind, not the other way around!"

"Doesn't matter," he said, though they both knew it did. "Just get your butt on the chopper."

She gritted her teeth. "I'm not going to the hospital when there's a crime scene to work."

"Let one of the others do it. Isn't that why the chief hired three of you? So there'd be redundancy in the Forensics Department?"

"No," Cassie said, neatly stepping between them. "He hired us because our skills complement each other, and because the BCCPD needed an upgrade." She turned her back on him and locked eyes with Alissa. "You should go with the girl. She'll need to talk to someone."

It was ironic that Cassie was playing the mediator. The tall, blond evidence specialist was usually the abrasive one, the sharp-tongued edgy one, who made enemies more easily than friends and never hesitated to express her opinion. If she was toning it down, it meant she'd been worried. Very worried.

Alissa clasped her friend's hand and smiled. "It'll be okay, but thanks." She glanced over and saw a petite, dark-haired figure climb into the helicopter. "Lizzie doesn't need me right now. Maya will help, and her parents will be waiting at the hospital. I'll go in later and see if I can get a sketch. For now I'll stay here and work the scene." She shot a look at Tucker, who stood nearby, glowering. "You got a problem with that?"

They both knew he did, and he probably had a point. She was tired and sore, and damned if her camera wasn't down there somewhere, amidst the busted-up ice and rock.

He scowled and turned away. "No problem. I'm not your keeper. Do what you need to do and leave me out of it."

And he was gone, taking the faint, lingering warmth with him.

Alissa watched him climb to the top of the canyon and work his way toward the back of the blown-out tunnel, where the bomb experts were already congregating. Then she held out a hand to Cassie. "Let me borrow your camera, okay? Mine's trash."

Cass cocked her head. "Want to talk about it?" She wasn't asking about what had happened in the tunnel.

Alissa shook her head. "Nothing to talk about. Let's do our jobs."

TUCKER WATCHED the two women work the scene together. There was no doubting they were a team. Cassie handled the evidence collection, having dragooned several task force members into digging, witnessing the collections, starting the chain of evidence and transporting the items back to a waiting vehicle.

Items. It sounded so much neater than bones, but that was what they were uncovering. A skeleton had been buried in a shallow grave at the side of the ice tunnel.

The searchers brought in heaters to melt the frost layer and used hand trowels, then brushes, to uncover the bones. The soil was bagged for sifting, and the bags were carefully labeled with exact coordinates.

Alissa helped when needed, but otherwise stood aside and recorded the process with photographs and detailed notes. She listed where each bone was found, how deep it was buried and how far away from the others. When the exhumation was complete, she could use her notes along with her new computer programs to recreate the scene in its entirety.

Which, Tucker admitted, would be a step up from Fitz's glossy photographs, and the hand-drawn schematics he used to tack on a flip board for the jury's view.

It wasn't that he had anything against progress, Tucker thought, as he watched Alissa record the position of a femur. And it wasn't as if he missed Fitz all that much. Hell, if the old coot wanted to retire, who was he to complain? It was...

Admit it, he muttered inwardly. *It's Alissa.*

She rattled him. Unsettled him. Fascinated him, though he had no business being fascinated with a local when he'd put in for—and been granted—his next transfer. The only thing keeping him in town right now was the task force. Once the girls were found and the kidnapper was in custody, he'd be in the wind.

Growing up, he'd hated the moves from one military base to the next, hated the look on his mother's face when his father's next set of orders came through. These days it was the opposite. His parents were happily settled in Arizona, while he was the one skipping around.

But he liked it that way. Liked his freedom. His independence.

As though she sensed his thoughts or his gaze, Alissa lowered the camera and looked across the distance separating them. He felt their eyes lock, felt a click of connection in his chest. He wanted to go to her, to tell her how he'd nearly gone out of his mind digging down to her.

Instead he turned away and focused on the second crime scene, where two members of the bomb squad were excavating what was left of the tunnel. Chief Parry stood nearby with his hands jammed in the pockets of his uniform parka. He frowned as Tucker joined him.

"Bastard rigged a trip wire to Lizzie's ankle and shoved her into the tunnel. We got a few fragments of the device. Trouper's taking them."

Tucker nodded. "Reasonable." The BCCPD had a good relationship with the feds, particularly the FBI. After the second kidnapping, when it became clear that this was more than a disgruntled teen hitting the road for Vegas or points west, they had called for help and gotten Trouper, a lean, graying agent who'd done his damnedest to help without stepping on toes.

Parry glanced over toward the rapidly emptying gravesite. "They find anything with the bones?"

Tucker shrugged. "More bones, maybe a few scraps of cloth. They're having trouble with the ice."

The chief grunted, which was his fallback answer to most everything. "The skeleton will go to the ME for a preliminary workup, and then we'll let Wyatt have the skull. Maybe we can get a recognizable face from it."

Tucker stuck his hands in his pockets. "Fitz said there was no way to reconstruct a face from a skull."

"Fitz also wasn't a big fan of blood-spatter trajectories and DNA. If it wasn't a fingerprint, he didn't want to know about it," Parry said with uncharacteristic asperity. "And I wish you guys would get off the Fitz kick already. You know as well as I do that he was a pain in the ass and long past retirement. Yeah, he cleared a hell of a lot of cases, but he was a damned dinosaur. You should be kissing these girls' butts for bringing in new techniques, not bitching because they do things differently. If they didn't, I wouldn't have hired them!"

The chief kept his voice low so they wouldn't be overheard, but there was no question that he was serious.

And knowing that the chief had a valid point, Tucker felt a low burn of shame. "But, Chief—"

"No buts. I want you with me on this." Parry leveled a finger at Tucker. "If you lead, the others will follow. I want you to give those women a break, particularly Wyatt."

Tucker shifted uneasily. "I don't have anything against Wyatt."

The captain grunted. "Baloney. You glare any time you're within fifty feet of her, and you do a damn good job of not letting that happen too often. Since you're usually a pretty level guy, I figure there's one of two reasons for that. Either you're hot for her or you hate her guts. Which is it?"

The chief's question hung on the air between them as the cold day dimmed toward a colder dusk. Tucker hid the wince—or tried to—and said, "Neither. I'm just not sure she's the right cop for the job. She's awfully young—" and tiny, delicate, breakable "—to be in charge of evidence collection."

"She's older than you were when you took the oath, McDermott. She has eight years on the job in Tecumseh, and more training than Fitz ever bothered to get." Parry shot him a look. "So what's your real problem with her?"

Knowing he wasn't going to win, Tucker set his teeth. "No problem, Chief."

"Good," Parry said in a voice that told Tucker he didn't believe a word of it. "Then you won't mind working with her on this case. You'll be good together—you see the big picture while she focuses on the details."

Damn, Tucker thought. He should've seen this coming a mile away. He shifted uncomfortably. "I don't think that's such a good idea."

"Well, I do, and that's what's important, isn't it?" Though Parry's voice remained quiet, his slate-blue eyes held a hint of steel in their depths. "I need her at the hospital to interview the girl. Go with her." Now a hint of frustration, of worry worked its way into the chief's expression. "I'm not doing this to ride your ass, McDermott. I need the team working together, and right now it's not. If we're not working together, we might not find this guy in time." Edgy concern snapped in his tone. "We might not find the other two girls in time."

Tucker felt it, too. The sense that an invisible timetable had been moved up by the kidnapper's mocking note. Was it simply a taunt, or did it mean something else?

Hell, he didn't know. And damned if the chief wasn't right—as usual. The task force needed to work together, not against itself. So Tucker nodded grudgingly. "Okay, I'll do it."

"Of course you will," Parry said. "It's an order."

ALISSA WAS STOWING her gear in Cassie's truck—and trying to hide the winces—when a strong arm grabbed her pack and Tucker's voice said, "You're riding with me."

She hated that, even after an afternoon as physically and emotionally bruising as this one, her pulse still kicked into overdrive at his nearness. Because of it, and because of the pounding aches in her back and neck, she turned and scowled at him. "You're kidding."

"Nope." He didn't look happy about it, either. "Chief Parry wants us together on this one. He wants us to go to the hospital and talk to Lizzie."

"That's where I'm headed," she snapped, "but not with you."

"Sorry." He slung her pack over his shoulder and gestured towards his vehicle—a black SUV with oversize tires and mud flaps emblazoned with the letters BCCPD. "Chief's orders. He wants his team working together on this."

"Oh." She tried not to slump as she understood. She, Cass and Maya hadn't been able to make friends, so the chief was going to do it for them. Damn, she hated being manipulated, hated that she hadn't been able to work it out on her own. Worse, she hated that part of her was excited at the idea of partnering with McDermott, even temporarily. Knowing it spelled trouble all the way around, she shook her head. "I can drive myself to the hospital and hook up with you later. There's no reason for us both to go—she might not even be conscious yet."

"True, but orders are orders." He slung her pack in the vehicle and left the passenger door ajar.

"Fine." She climbed stiffly into the SUV.

As they drove out of Bear Creek State Forest, she felt the sore spots burn and pound, felt her muscles stiffen up. She'd gone from being trapped under hundreds of pounds of rocks and dirt directly to working the scene. She'd refused to go to the hospital with Lizzie because the other victims needed her more than she'd needed medical attention.

Now, a soft bed and some aspirin was sounding real good.

When McDermott blasted the heat, she expelled a grateful sigh, let her head fall back against the seat and closed her eyes.

And opened them right up again, because the first thing she'd seen in her tired brain was a small patch of yellow flashlight beam and a wall of dirt six inches from her face. She shuddered at the memory.

"I've got the heat as high as it'll go."

She glanced at him, then away, trying to ignore how intimate the area seemed as the dusk faded to night. "I didn't say anything."

And she didn't say anything else until he pulled up

in front of the small house she'd leased for a year, with the option to buy if everything worked out with the BCCPD.

She stared at the lit front entryway, battling the urge to bolt inside, jump into bed and wish the whole day away. "I thought we were going to the hospital to interview Lizzie."

That was where she wanted to go. Needed to go. Not just to do her job, but also to reassure herself that the girl was alive. To thank her, ironically, for being human company beneath the ice and snow. If it hadn't been for the feeling of Lizzie's ankle beneath her fingertips, Alissa thought she might have lost it completely.

"We are," he said. "But you need to take a shower first. Or at least change clothes and wash your face. You'll terrify the poor kid if you show up looking like that."

His voice held a tone of censure, and something else. Something darker and more dangerous, that sent a skitter of awareness shooting through her body.

With a start, she realized he hadn't asked for directions. He'd known where she lived.

She wondered what it meant, and then decided probably nothing. He was a cop. He knew his neighborhoods.

"Yeah. You've got a point." And, God, would it feel good to soak her bones in the Jacuzzi tub that had sold her on the house. Since there wasn't time for a bath, she'd settle for a fast shower, but it'd help.

She pushed open the door and stifled a groan as her

weary legs went rubbery. Since there was no way she was asking McDermott for help, she forced some strength into her body and shuffled into the house. All the way, she was too aware of him following, not close enough to crowd, but close enough to catch her if she fell.

She felt his presence there in the little prickles of electricity on her skin, in the subtle warmth in her core, and was reminded of another time, when they'd followed each other out of the club with no other thought than to get naked, damn the consequences.

Only, he hadn't damned the consequences. He'd bailed the moment he'd realized she was a cop and a co-worker. Part of her was grateful he'd had the strength. Part of her still yearned for the sizzle. And the whole of her was ashamed that she'd nearly given in to something as pointless as lust with a man who—according to PD rumor—already had one foot out the door.

Been there, done that. Don't need to do it again, no matter how hot he is, she told herself.

Inside the house, she waved him to the kitchen and ignored the oddness of seeing him standing there, in her space. "Food and drinks are in the fridge—take whatever appeals. Guest bath is at the end of the hall. I'll be five minutes, no more."

When she'd picked the house, she'd loved the convenience of having everything on one floor. Now it seemed like a disadvantage. A vulnerability. Even once she was inside the master bath, with its Jacuzzi tub and sybaritic adjoining lounge, she felt exposed.

She stripped naked and jumped into the shower fast, hissing at the sting of water on bruises and scrapes, then nearly moaning as the warmth eased some of the pain. But she didn't dally. She had five minutes to shower and dress and get the hell on the road to the hospital.

She had a witness to interview. A murderer to sketch.

Two missing girls to find.

Chapter Three

At the Hawthorne Memorial Hospital, Alissa and McDermott were ID'd twice, once at the main desk and once again as they approached the private room where Lizzie lay. Though the kidnapper had left her as bait, there was no telling whether or not he'd try to get her back. Frankly there was no telling much of anything yet.

The whole case was clear as mud, Alissa thought, as she followed McDermott down the hall. The kidnapper appeared to have a plan, but what was it? Would the other girls reappear one at a time? Or were they already dead? Was he using the girls to get to the police—as the canyon attack suggested—or vice versa?

At the door to Lizzie's hospital room, Alissa held up a hand. "I'm going in alone."

"No way." McDermott scowled, and the overhead lights darkened his deep-brown eyes to nearly black. "Remember what Parry said? We're working together on this."

"But he didn't say we needed to be joined at the hip, did he?" She lifted her chin and ignored the fine buzz that ran across her skin at his nearness. "I'm going in alone. I'm betting she'll be more relaxed with a woman than a man, and the more she relaxes, the more I'll be able to get out of her."

Not waiting for him to argue, she opened the door, stepped through and shut it in his face. Then she breathed through her mouth in an exaggerated sigh of stress. Frustration.

She wished she knew Chief Parry better, wished she knew whether it was safe to complain to him. Because there was no doubt in her mind that she and McDermott working together was a bad idea. They were just going to annoy each other.

Distract each other.

"You okay?"

The question startled her, because it came in a very familiar voice. "Maya!"

"Who else did you expect?" The dark-haired beauty unfolded herself from a chair beside the bed, which held the blond pixie that Alissa knew from her picture.

Sixteen-year-old Elizabeth Walsh, taken from the MovieMogul parking lot by a man in a light-colored van. And now, miraculously, home safe.

Or so Alissa hoped.

Almost afraid to ask, she glanced at Maya. "Is she ...?"

"She seems generally okay—bumps, bruises, exposure and hypothermia, but nothing else." The BCCFD's forensic psychologist—and counselor—touched the sleeping girl's wrist. "She's been in and out. Her parents and younger brother have been here for the past few hours. I just sent them off for a snack and a walk."

Maya's long-lashed eyes were dark with sympathy. Alissa knew the family couldn't be in better hands. Maya had a way with victims and suspects, just as Alissa had a way with scenes, and Cassie with evidence.

The three made a strong unit, stronger even than the retired Fitz, who had left before they arrived, not bothering to help ease their transition onto the force. Alissa gritted her teeth. Well, to hell with him. To hell with men in general. She was here to do a job, not make new friends.

"Can you intercept the parents?" she asked Maya. "I'd like some time alone with her."

"Sure. I'll speak with them about easing her back into her normal life and dealing with the aftermath. They've asked about counseling, so I'm hopeful that we'll be able to help her move on." The warning in Maya's eyes was velvet gentleness over a core of steel. *Don't mess up her head.*

But how could Alissa promise that? She needed the young woman—little more than a child, really, she was so small and fragile looking—to remember things she would probably rather forget. In the long run, it would help her …but the short run was going to hurt.

"I'll do my best," Alissa answered, though they both knew it wasn't really an answer at all.

Maya, being Maya, smiled and touched her arm in

passing. "I know you will, 'Lissa." She turned back with her hand on the door. "You want me to send one of the boys to sit outside the door and make sure you have your privacy?"

"Already taken care of," Alissa said. "McDermott's outside." Then she held a finger to her lips and mouthed, *and he's probably listening.*

Lord knows she would be, under the same circumstances.

Maya raised her eyebrows but didn't comment beyond a cautious, "Okay. I'll be back to check on you in twenty."

"Good enough." Alissa watched as Maya pushed through the door. Sure enough, McDermott was right outside, not even bothering to pretend he wasn't eavesdropping.

She glared and he flicked an unrepentant half-smile. Then the door swung shut between them, separating them some, but not enough. Irritated and faintly anxious, she forced her mind back on to the job. On to the girl, the victim who had seen the face of her kidnapper.

Or so Alissa hoped.

She pulled out her pad and turned back to the bed, intending to sit with Lizzie until she woke up. But the girl's eyes were open and wary. "I already told them I don't remember anything," Lizzie said, voice faintly petulant, as though Alissa was interrupting her.

"Okay." Alissa sat and settled her sketch pad in her lap. When she lifted the hard charcoal pencil she used for initial blocking work, she saw the girl's eyes follow. "We'll just chat a little until your parents come back. No pressure."

Instead of tarting off or repeating her denial, Lizzie surprised Alissa.

The girl began to cry.

Huge tears welled up in her eyes and spilled over, and she rolled to her side and hugged her knees to her chest beneath the thin hospital blanket. "I th-thought he was going to kill me. He said he was going to, that I wouldn't have any warning. That one night he'd just do it, maybe while I was sleeping." She swallowed a racking sob. "I t-tried not to sleep much after that, but it was so cold. So dark. Once, I woke up and he was standing over me. He had a knife." She burrowed her face into the pillow and howled, straining her body into the mattress as though she wished it would swallow her up. "Then he put me in that cave. He drugged me. I was out of it, but I knew what he'd done. I knew there was a bomb. I thought I was going to die when you came. I thought we were both dead."

Her thin frame shuddered with the force of her tears.

Alissa's throat closed, and she reached out to touch the girl's scraped-raw ankle, the only part of Lizzie she could reach from her seat.

God, she hated this. She wanted to gather the young woman in her arms and tell her not to think about it. Instead she forced her voice calm and asked about the place where Lizzie had been held. About the man, who'd always stayed in the shadows. About what he'd said, what he'd done. What he'd looked like.

Lizzie cried as she talked. The words came pouring out of her as though she'd wanted to talk about it, *needed* to talk about it, even though she'd said she remembered nothing.

But she remembered, all right. She remembered plenty, though maybe not enough. As she talked, Alissa sketched furiously, trusting her microcorder to catch all of the girl's descriptions for later analysis. The images engraved themselves on her heart, wounding her with fear for the others, for herself.

After ten minutes Lizzie's words slowed. After fifteen, they stopped altogether and the girl slipped back to sleep, her body shutting down when her soul couldn't handle any more.

Instead of being frustrated, Alissa was grateful. She wasn't sure she could have handled more, herself. So she sighed, swiped her sleeve across both cheeks where sympathetic tears had dried and pushed to her feet. The outer door moved slightly as she crossed the room, but by the time she opened it, McDermott was leaning against the far wall, looking like he'd been there all along.

She jerked her head towards the exit. "Come on. Let's talk to the task force."

Instead of moving right away, he stared at her, dark eyes intense, until she raised a hand to her cheek, expecting to find that she'd missed a tear. Then he uncoiled and crossed to her. He stopped a breath away, and the warmth of his body eased the tension inside her chest even as it tightened another, lower down.

He started to say something and stopped. Started again and stopped. Then he blew out a breath and said simply, "If we're going to be working together, I suppose you should call me Tucker."

Surprise rattled through the numbness left by her painful sketch session, and she nodded. "Thanks. I'm Alissa."

Sneaky pleasure warmed her. It wasn't quite acceptance, wasn't quite a pat on the back for how she'd handled Lizzie.

But it was a start.

STILL FEELING GUT PUNCHED by what he'd overheard of Alissa's interview with the rescued girl, Tucker ushered her down the hall toward the exit. He was careful not to touch her, because if he did, he might pull her into his arms and tell her that it was okay, that she'd done the right thing by questioning the witness, by keeping her talking.

He'd seen the self-doubt in her eyes, seen what the interview had taken out of her.

They passed a small, intimate waiting area that was painted in soothing blues and golds. The psych specialist, Maya, sat there with Lizzie's mother, father and brother, all of whom looked exhausted and haggard but happier than he'd seen them in the weeks since the kidnapping.

Tucker nodded as the family stood and filtered back toward the hospital room on Maya's heels, all save for Lizzie's father, a shaved-bald patriarch who stank of the cigarettes he'd chain-smoked while they waited for news.

Reginald Walsh stopped near Alissa and said in a low voice, "I don't care what it takes. I want you to get the bastard. Find him."

A few of the officers had reported having problems with Walsh, who operated used-car lots around the city and seemed to think money should be enough to buy his daughter home. The morning after her kidnapping, he'd thrown a chair through the front window of his house when one of the officers had suggested Lizzie might have run away.

Knowing this, Tucker stepped between Walsh and Alissa. "We're working on it. You take care of your daughter and your family. We'll take care of finding and punishing her kidnapper."

He kept his voice low but stared the guy in his blood-shot eyes. The last thing they needed right now was a vigilante out for justice.

Walsh glared. "I don't give a damn about punishing the bastard right now. Not yet. That'll come later. Right now, I just care about finding those girls for their families." His voice went strangled. "For God's sake, they're just kids."

He pushed past Tucker, who felt a punch of shame at having misjudged the man. On the heels of shame came fatigue. He'd been up nearly thirty hours without a break, and the last few had been a hell of a ride.

"Hey, Tucker. You okay?" Alissa asked, concern darkening her blue eyes. A wisp of hair slipped from its twist and brushed across her forehead, making her look soft and vulnerable.

Her use of his first name echoed back to that night, when they'd been Alissa and Tucker, and they'd danced close enough that they might have been inside each other's skins. Ever since they'd been reintroduced through the BCCPD, he'd been McDermott and she'd been Wyatt.

It shouldn't have made a difference. But because it did, and because he was tired and feeling a little mean, he turned away and headed for the exit. "I'm fine. Come on, let's get out of here."

He didn't need to look to know that she had his back. He could feel her presence like a slow-burning fire in his nerve endings, one that reminded him of his transfer request. He'd be gone as soon as this case was wrapped up, and she'd be staying in her roomy, family-friendly house. The house alone should be enough to make him back off.

So how come every time he meant to back off, he seemed to take a step closer?

IT WAS COMPLETELY DARK when Alissa and Tucker made it back to the PD, but most of the task-force members were there, looking tired, haggard, and rundown by too many questions and not enough answers.

Maya hadn't returned from the hospital yet, but Cassie had saved their seats, as usual. Alissa felt a small pang, as though she was abandoning Tucker when he took his customary position against the back wall. He'd been broody and curt during the ride from the hospital, but his mood seemed to have gained a layer of desperation that made her nervous.

It was as though he was reaching the end of his endurance in some way, though she didn't think it was physical. It was more like he was pushing himself to a mental brink.

On a professional level, she didn't think it was good for the case. On a personal level, she wished she could help but knew she didn't have the right to press. He'd made that perfectly clear when he'd bailed out of her car that night at the club. Tucker was a no-relationships kind of guy.

Heck, at least he'd been honest about it.

She tried to convince herself she was grateful as she took her seat. One look at Cassie turned her thoughts in an entirely new direction. "What's wrong?"

Her first unsettling thought was that there'd been a breach in the chain of evidence. But the anger in Cass's sky-blue eyes seemed more personal than that, the scowl on her face more directed when she said, "Trouper is threatening to bring in a new guy, an evidence tech from the FBI, to *help* me." She stressed the word as if it was poison. "I don't need help. I'm already doing everything that can be done."

Alissa tried to shift her brain into this new gear, tried to sympathize with Cass, who could be territorial when it came to her lab. "Well …does this guy have access to equipment you don't? Can he get you into the federal databanks more quickly?" She took a breath, thought about the blond pixie in the hospital bed and exhaled. "I don't think we can let this be about a power struggle. It's about finding the other girls and catching the kidnapper."

Cassie winced and looked faintly ashamed. "You're right. I know you're right, it's just …this whole thing has me unsettled. I talked to the new guy, Seth Varitek, on the phone, and I already don't like him. He's pushy. He…crowds me. And besides, I hate that it feels like us versus them on this case. If I'm protecting my back from the good guys, then who's going to be looking for the bad guy?"

"It's not that bad," Alissa said, thinking Cassie was overreacting and wondering whether there was more to the story. But before she could ask, Maya slipped in through the back door and Chief Parry stepped to the front of the room, ready to start the meeting.

"Good work today, people." Parry looked to the back of the room, where Alissa could feel Tucker's presence like a disturbance in the air. Then the chief's eyes moved to her and on to the others. "Elizabeth Walsh is safe and sound, and has already been through a round of interviews. However—" he sobered, his eyes going hard "—both the victim and Officer Wyatt were nearly killed today by an explosive device we presume was set by the kidnapper. We were led to the site by a note addressed to Detective McDermott."

Though the twenty or so cops on the task force already knew the details, a rumbling murmur ran through the room. A slick-haired veteran named

Piedmont, who always found reasons to avoid greeting Alissa in the hallway, glanced over at her with less than the usual dose of venom in his glare. "He's playing with us."

"Yeah. He's playing with us." Chief Parry let the silence linger a beat too long before he said, "So let's end the game. Let's find him." He gestured to Alissa. "Wyatt will start us off with her report."

She felt twenty-plus pairs of eyes on her, felt the bruises on her cheek and chin throb, and forced herself to stand tall. Always before, she'd given her report to a sea of glowers or studied disinterest. This time the room felt slightly different. A hair less hostile. Maybe even a little bit ashamed.

A bubble of irony lodged in her throat. Either Chief Parry had succeeded with his plan to partner her with McDermott, or else the best way to catch a break with her new co-workers was to nearly get herself killed on the job.

Whatever. Resolved to follow her own advice to Cassie and focus on the case rather than office politics, Alissa squared her shoulders and made her report. "Pendelton is copying a sketch for me. Elizabeth said—" she fumbled slightly as the memory of the girl's sobs tore through her "—Lizzie was able to give me a partial description of the suspect and the place where she was held. He kept her in a small, single room made of wood. She thought it was one of those prefab sheds, the kind you can get at a garden store."

She could almost feel a collective indrawn breath at

the new information. Chief Parry pointed to a pair of homicide detectives. "Piedmont. You and Mendoza follow up on that. Get me lists of the local distributors and their customers, especially multiple orders. Maybe we'll get lucky."

It would be a huge list. But it would be a start.

Alissa glanced at her notes and continued, "Lizzie was given unwrapped energy bars and two-liter bottles of diet soda every few days." Which could mean that that her captor wasn't on the premises 24/7. "She heard wind and birds, creaking trees. No motor noises or other human beings, though she says that he drugged her at least once. Most important, she could hear the other girls. As of yesterday morning, they were both alive."

A ripple of energy ran through the room at the news. New purpose. Strengthened determination. They had to find those girls.

"As for Lizzie's captor," Alissa spread her hands, "I did my best, but she was understandably distraught." And putting the girl through the description had made her feel faintly slimy, as though some of the evil had rubbed off on them both. There was motion at the back of the room as the door opened and the desk clerk passed a stack of pages to McDermott. Alissa gestured, "As you'll see from the sketches Tuck—Detective McDermott—is passing around, our suspect is a white male, under six feet tall, with a round head, either bald or wearing a skull cap. Lizzie said he didn't talk much, and when he did, exclusively to threaten her, he pitched his voice in a low growl."

She saw the other officers frowning over her sketch and felt a slide of professional embarrassment. "I'm sorry it's not more detailed. I'll talk with her again tomorrow, and I'll reinterview her friends, the ones who might have seen the guy outside the MovieMogul 10."

But instead of the eye rolls and sneers she half expected, she got nods and eye contact. Tracy Mendoza, Piedmont's partner and another of the less-than-welcoming cops, said, "It's more than we had earlier. Thanks."

It wasn't until the rumble of agreement rolled over the room that Alissa realized how uncomfortable she'd been since starting work at the BCCPD.

And how much the faintest hint of acceptance meant to her.

She retook her seat on numb legs as Chief Parry called on Cassie to discuss the skeleton and the explosive device, both excavated from the ice tunnel.

The room cooled back to studied indifference or outright hostility as Cassie swaggered up to the front, chipped shoulder firmly in place. "Lizzie's clothing is next on my list for examination, but a preliminary scan suggests we won't get much. Between the wet and the dirt from the tunnel, it's going to be tough to tell the trace evidence from the rest. The explosive-device fragments have been forwarded to an FBI expert." She didn't acknowledge Trouper and she certainly didn't look happy about the interdepartmental cooperation as she continued, "and the skeleton has gone to the ME for examination. A preliminary scan indicates that we exhumed a complete skeleton, with a couple of the smaller bones missing. No cause of death was immediately apparent." She shrugged. "We'll know more in a day or so."

Chief Parry frowned. "How quickly can you get the skull to Wyatt for facial reconstruction?"

"She'll have it first thing tomorrow."

"Good. See that she does." Parry waved Cassie back to her seat and called another officer to report.

The rest of the meeting amounted to a whole lot of negatives. The suspects questioned to date all had solid alibis, including Lizzie's neighbor, Bradford Croft, whose name had dinged on the sex offender registry, making him an immediate suspect. A few other names were kicked around, including a longtime local named Michael Swopes, who had a string of low-level juvenile priors, and had done custom cabinet work for the families of the first and third kidnap victims.

It was near 10:00 p.m. when Parry closed the meeting. "Okay, people. Night shift, you know what you're doing. Day shift, go home and get some rest." His eyes slid to Alissa. "You all look like you could use it."

No kidding, she thought. The aches of the day sang through her body and left her nearly limp. But she forced herself to her feet and headed for the door. Cassie and Maya stayed behind to talk to Captain Parry, but Alissa couldn't bear to wait for them. She wanted food, aspirin and her bed, not necessarily in that order.

She was so tired that she wasn't even surprised to see

Tucker waiting for her out in the hallway. "You want a ride home?" he asked.

A ride home, a shoulder to lean on. Hell, even just a hug. Yeah, she could use all that. And because she wanted it so badly, she shook her head. "I'm fine." When he fell into step beside her, she slanted him a look. "I said I'm fine, Tucker. Shift's over. You don't have to play nice with me anymore on Chief's orders."

They exited out to the shadowed parking lot, where the number of personal cars sitting beneath the sodium lights attested to the big case. The cop shop wouldn't sleep until the girls were home—safe, God willing— and the kidnapper was in custody.

Tucker growled low in his throat. "Don't be a pain. You're all done in and I don't think you should be driving." He waved to his SUV. "Get in. I'll pick you up in the morning."

She turned to face him, noting how the bare lighting threw his hard-cut features into stark relief and darkened his eyes to jet. When he stepped closer—too close—she felt a tug of nerves. "Look. I appreciate the concern, but I'm fine. I don't need a babysitter, okay?"

They stared at each other for a beat before he dipped his head. At first, she had the insane notion that he was going to kiss her. At the thought heat blazed through her body, a raging, unwise, uncaring inferno that recalled the flash and flame they'd created together once before.

Then she realized he was only nodding. "I got it." His voice rasped on the words, as though he was restraining a curse, or something else.

He stepped back, and she felt as if they'd just ended an embrace, though they hadn't touched. Her lips were tender and swollen as though they had kissed. Her body revved and begged as though they had done even more than that.

He lifted an eyebrow. "You going or not? If you fall asleep on your feet in the middle of the parking lot, I'll be obliged to drive you home."

"I'm going." She spun blindly and nearly tripped over her own feet as she hurried to her VW, painfully aware of her own thoughts, and painfully certain he'd read them in her face. Why else had his eyes been dark, his expression cloaked with a fierceness that bordered on passion?

She fumbled for her keys and unlocked her car, only then noticing a single sheet of paper trapped beneath the wiper blade. Thinking it was a menu, or a flier for the grunge club down the street, she grabbed for it.

The block-lettered words took a moment to register. *You're getting warmer.*

She heard a click and saw a curl of plastic-coated wire beneath her wiper blade. She turned to run and scream a warning, but her feet moved in slow motion and her voice failed her.

She heard another click. A dull *whump!* of detonation.

Something hit her from behind, driving her to the ground and pressing her flat.

And the night erupted in searing, choking flames.

Chapter Four

Tucker hit the pavement between two parked cars on his knees and elbows and tried not to squash Alissa flat. Then the world exploded, and flat was the only option.

He gritted his teeth and clung to her, curled around her as the wall of concussion slammed into him and left him limp. The heated air crisped his clothes and skin, and the roar of explosion nearly deafened him.

The windows blew out of the nearby cars. Chips of glass slashed down on the back of his neck, into his hair, and his left leg burned like hell.

Adrenaline hammered through him, fear for himself, for her. Secondary detonations sounded and he braced for added heat before he realized that nearby car tires were blowing out, overpressurized by expanding air.

Then the main explosion rolled over and passed. The heat dimmed slightly, the roaring receded, and other sounds took over. Crackling flames. Shouts.

He felt the burn of hot cloth across his back and legs,

the body of the woman beneath him, and the knowledge battered at his brain.

Someone had tried to kill her. The trap hadn't been anonymous this time, hadn't been baited with a kidnapped girl that any one of them would have gone after. Alissa's car had been rigged to blow, which meant one of two things—either the kidnapper had watched them in the canyon and seen the explosion and the escape…or Alissa had an enemy of her own.

Aware of the fading heat and the low-throated roar of hand-held fire extinguishers, of shouts and approaching footsteps, Tucker levered himself to the side. His body parts all worked the way they were supposed to, and even the burning pain in his calf was fading to manageable levels. He reached out to touch Alissa, but she moved before he could rouse her. She rolled to her side, facing him.

Her eyes were stark in her pale face, which was cast orangey-red by the flicker of nearby flames. Shock hadn't set in yet, or if it had, she was holding it at bay with force of will.

Her lips trembled, then shaped three words. "We're getting warmer." His first insane thought was that she was trying to joke about nearly having been killed. Then she shifted to sit up, swaying, and shoved a crumpled piece of paper at him. "The bastard sends his greetings."

Tucker sat up and grabbed the paper, automatically handling it by the edges, though there was little hope of getting usable evidence from it.

You're getting warmer.

Tucker cursed as their suspicions were confirmed. The kidnapper was playing a game with the cops. But to what end?

"Here they are!" Mendoza's voice shouted. Footsteps thundered toward the narrow gap between two cars, where Tucker and Alissa had taken shelter from the blast.

Cassie and Maya were at the front of the group, panicky and frantic looking. But instead of letting them fuss over Alissa, Tucker climbed stiffly to his feet and offered her a hand. The bulk of his body blocked the space between the two cars, creating a small, intimate area for just the two of them.

Surprise showed in her tired, shadowed eyes, and she put her hand in his. The shimmer of contact was a slow, sexy burn he didn't know how to handle, any more than he knew how to deal with the bright sizzle of anger and fear he felt at the situation, at the bastard who'd tried to kill her twice that day.

He pulled Alissa gently to her feet, giving her time to veto the move if she was hurt. But the glint in her eye and the set to her delicate, feminine jaw told him that, like him, she had little intention of admitting to an injury.

It surprised him to realize they had something in common, after all.

Then he got a second shock when her eyes softened to nearly the openness they'd held that night at the bar, when she'd looked at him like a woman looks at a man when she likes what she sees. She tightened her fingers on his hand. "Thank you." She glanced over his shoulder and must have seen the growing crowd beyond their small space, because she flushed and dropped his hand. But then she looked back into his eyes as though steeling herself for a difficult conversation. "I owe you one. Two, really. One for digging me out earlier, and one for just now when…" She faltered, swallowed and then continued, "If you hadn't knocked me down, I would've been toast. Literally. So, thanks."

Nearby, a fire truck's wail increased, then quit when the vehicle rolled into the parking lot and stopped beside the charred remains of her VW.

Tucker eased away and tucked his scraped hands into his pockets, which were still warm. If he'd learned anything about Alissa Wyatt in the time she'd been at the BCCPD, it was that she didn't bend easily, didn't apologize easily and didn't want to owe anybody anything, except perhaps, her two closest friends.

Knowing that the gratitude was hard for her, and realizing that this was another thing they might have in common, he simply nodded. "That's what partners are for."

Then he stepped aside and gestured her out from between the cars toward the waiting crowd. Cassie and Maya grabbed her and hustled her to an ambulance parked behind the fire truck. Tucker felt a ghost of amusement as her protests rose over the hiss of water and foam, the ticking of hot metal and violence. Then he refocused and sought out Chief Parry in the crowd.

The chief wasn't hard to find. He was huddled over the VW's engine compartment with Sawyer, who headed the bomb squad. Both men looked up when Tucker approached.

"You look like hell," the chief said without preamble. "Go see the paramedics."

"I'm fine." Tucker handed over the sheet of paper. "You'll want to enter this into evidence. It was pinned under Alissa's windshield wiper."

Parry's eyes sharpened on the single line, and he cursed. "So, there's no question about it. Same guy."

"Same guy," Tucker echoed. He glanced at Sawyer. "Anything on the device?"

The grizzled bomb expert, who'd been one of Fitz's closest friends on the force, shrugged equivocally. "It's fried and scattered. Won't know much until we've really been over this place."

"Do you think it was the same guy?" Tucker persisted, knowing that Sawyer didn't like to draw early conclusions, but sure he already knew the answer.

Sawyer glanced at the chief. "Could be."

Which was as good as a *yes* in Sawyer-speak.

Tucker turned to the chief. "We're going to need to—"

Parry held up a hand. "I've got it under control, *Detective*." He stressed the last word, making it clear that Tucker wasn't in charge here, and—as the chief had made painfully clear one night over beers—never would be if he kept transferring every few years. He jerked his chin toward the ambulance. "Get yourself checked out and go home. You've been up for nearly seventy-two hours. You're no use to me until you're rested."

Tucker scowled and turned away, knowing his boss was right but not liking it. But Parry's voice called, "McDermott!"

Tucker turned back. "Yeah?"

The chief lifted the single sheet of paper. "I'll put a man on your place and one on Wyatt's. You two are the only ones who've gotten notes."

"I know." And while part of him was excited about the contact with the kidnapper, the rest of him hated it. Not for his sake, but for Alissa's.

Tucker knew he could take care of himself. He wasn't sure about the new crime-scene specialist, though. She tried to play it tough, but she was too delicate. Too fragile. Too easy to crush with the next cave-in, the next explosion. And that worried the hell out of him, not just because she was a woman and a cop, but because he liked her, damn it. He'd tried not to, but there it was. She had guts. Spunk. And a hell of a pair of legs, though that shouldn't have mattered.

And he wouldn't let it, he told himself. This was about a cop in danger, not about sex or the way she'd felt about him when they danced. So he jammed his hands into his pockets and nodded to Parry. "I'll keep an eye on her. She's my partner, after all."

At least for as long as he was in town.

ALISSA LOVED HER FRIENDS, but sometimes they drove her up a wall. Like now.

"I'm said I'm fine!" She glared at Cassie and Maya, who had her backed up against the fire truck. "The paramedics believed me, why won't you?"

She *was* fine, for the moment. The adrenaline from the attack buzzed in her bloodstream, keeping her on her feet. She would crash hard later, but she wasn't ready to drop yet. More important, she didn't want to lose it in public. Hell, she didn't even want her friends to see. Some things were best kept private, like weakness.

Cassie's eyes narrowed. "Because we know you. And because—"

Maya held up a hand to stop Cassie's words, which were gaining volume and pitch. "And because we love you, 'Lissa. We worry about you."

Aw, heck. Tears pressed against the back of Alissa's eyes and her throat tightened. She could usually stand up to Cassie's brazenness, but Maya's gentle compassion did her in. How long had it been since she'd let herself really lean on someone else?

A long time, she thought. She'd loved Aiden—at least until he'd gotten his dream sportscaster job and taken off with little regret—but she'd never needed to depend on him. And before that? It had been her against the world most of the time. Her against the bill collectors her mother could never quite keep up with. Her against her studies, then her academy training, where she'd always felt the need to be tougher than the others when she wasn't bigger; smarter than the others when she wasn't faster.

Then Maya made it worse by stepping forward and wrapping her arms around Alissa in a hug. The petite, dark-haired counselor whispered, "You don't have to do it all yourself. Cassie and I aren't leaving you. We're not going anywhere."

Alissa nearly howled, *Damn it, Maya, not here!* She was in the middle of the parking lot, with cops all around her. She'd just barely made a dent in the wall of resentment they carried against her—the last thing she needed to do was blubber in front of them. So she bit the inside of her cheek and pulled away with a choked, "Thanks, Maya. But right now, I just want to go home."

"I'll take you," a voice said from behind her. Tucker's familiar masculine tones rubbed raw against her fragile defenses, nearly panicking her with an overwhelming urge to throw herself at him. She remembered regaining consciousness earlier that day and finding herself in his arms. In that weak, vulnerable moment between conscious and not, she'd felt safe, protected.

Comforted.

Danger! her brain screamed. *Bad idea!* Tucker McDermott wasn't what she wanted or needed. After Aiden had taken off, she'd made a mental list of what she wanted in her next man. The first line said simply, "Must have roots."

Tucker was a self-confessed traveler, like Aiden. Like her father. She'd be a fool to get involved with him.

So she fought back the tears, stiffened her spine and turned to him. "No, thanks. I'll have one of the girls run me home."

Maya's too-tender concern was definitely preferable to a six-foot-plus temptation named McDermott.

"Not good enough," he said flatly, his tone brooking no argument.

But that didn't deter Cassie, who seemed to be itching for a fight. Maybe it was the stress of the day, Alissa thought, the incidents with the bombs or the threat of an FBI evidence tech honing in on her turf. Or maybe there was something else going on with Cass, because when she stepped forward and got in Tucker's face, there was a glint of desperation in her blue eyes. "What do you mean we're not good enough? We're cops just like you, buster. Don't you dare tell us we're not good enough!"

Tucker's eyes darkened to near black, and he clenched his jaw. Alissa could nearly feel the impatience and anger pulsing off of him in sharp, hot waves. She braced herself for an explosion, for the volatile McDermott she'd heard about but never witnessed firsthand.

Instead he kept his tone level when he said, "I never said you weren't good enough. I said your *plan* wasn't good enough. Alissa doesn't need to be dropped off at home, she needs protection. Or have you forgotten that the car bomb was specifically aimed at her? The bastard has targeted her, one way or another." While the word *targeted* banged around in Alissa's overworked brain, Tucker took a step forward and managed to loom over Cassie, though she was only a few inches shorter than he. "And while you may be a cop, you're an evidence specialist, not a street detective. No offense, but I'd take me over you on a protection detail any day."

"And you're a guy," Cassie snapped. "Don't tell me that macho bull doesn't factor into it."

"Enough!" Alissa said, head spinning, tears not far off. "Both of you knock it off."

She was aware of Maya standing back, out of the fray, watching with sad eyes. Not for the first time she wondered what it was that Maya didn't like to talk about, what had made her a quiet, introspective woman who occasionally showed a quirky flash of mischief, as though there was a whole second person behind those deep-brown eyes. But this wasn't about Maya, it was about Cassie and Alissa. And Tucker.

Adrenaline starting to drain, Alissa stepped between Cassie and Tucker when she would have rather run for her car. Except that her car was gone, and she had nowhere to run to.

The word *targeted* whispered in her soul. Was it true? Had the kidnapper set his sights on her?

Realizing the combatants were both staring at her, she took a deep breath. Then let it out again. Hell, she didn't know what she wanted.

"I don't need protection," she found herself saying, though the bravado seemed patently untrue.

"Yes, you do," Tucker countered with a hint of steel in his voice. "That bomb was meant for you."

Cold nerves shivered down her spine, but she turned to him, effectively shutting Cassie out of the conversation. "You got a note, too. What's to say the charge in the tunnel wasn't meant for you?"

His eyes darkened with irritation, or maybe something else. "It probably was meant for me, which makes us both targets. That's why we need to watch each other's backs." The corner of his mouth kicked up in a sardonic smile. "Chief's orders."

"Oh," Alissa said, when she really wanted to say, *Oh, hell.* Parry seemed intent on dumping the two of them together for the sake of the BCCPD. He had no idea of their history. No idea that her heart pounded and her mouth went dry in McDermott's presence.

And she had no intention of letting anyone know that little fact. Especially not Tucker.

"Shall we?" He gestured to his SUV, which had remained outside the blast radius, unscathed. His eyes reminded her that she'd have been safer if she'd accepted his offer of a ride in the first place.

Or would she have been? Danger, it seemed, came in many forms.

"Fine." She turned to Maya and Cassie, who now stood shoulder to shoulder with identical worried looks on their faces. "I'll see you guys in the morning. Get some sleep."

Cassie glared at Tucker. "You'll take care of her?"

Irritated, Alissa opened her mouth to snap that nobody needed to "take care" of her, but he clamped a hand on her upper arm and said, "Everything's under control. We'll see you tomorrow."

He turned her and marched her to the SUV while her brain grappled with one simple word. *We.*

He loaded her into the passenger seat and shut the door for her before she could even think to protest. They were on the road in moments. She sat and stared out the window, feeling numb shock start to take over her body, her consciousness.

We. How long had it been since she'd truly been part of a *we,* one that made her feel stronger rather than weaker? She'd thought that she and Aiden had been a pair, but once the dust of his departure had settled, she'd realized their relationship had been less about partners and more about convenience and appearances. He'd been a network TV up-and-comer, and dating a cop had played well with his bosses. Heck, she'd admit that it hadn't hurt her reputation at the Tecumseh PD that she was dating a hunky jock sportscaster.

Things had seemed great until the rape trial, when the tainted evidence was excluded and scuzzy Johnny Ferguson was acquitted. Though it had been her partner's mistake, Alissa's name had taken a hit from the irate community. Hurt, she had turned to Aiden for comfort.

And he had withdrawn. He was gone not long after. Just like a man, he'd taken off when things had gone from fun to complicated.

Unexpectedly, horrifyingly, Alissa's eyes filled. Too conscious of McDermott's solid presence in the driver's seat, she turned her face to the window and swiped at the tears, hoping he wouldn't notice.

No such luck. With a quiet curse, he pulled over to the side of the road, set the brake and jumped out of the SUV. For a moment she thought he was giving her privacy. Then he pulled open her door. "Hop out. We're going for a walk."

Too tired to argue, too miserable to ask why, she popped her seat belt and climbed down. They had stopped near a trailhead of the Bear Claw State Park, where a finger of conservation land broke up the carefully sculpted housing developments. This late at night, Tucker's vehicle was alone in the parking lot, and the only sign of civilization was the twinkle of house lights reflecting on the far side of an iced-over lake.

"Come on." He led her to the side of the trail, down a windy, overgrown path that she could barely see in the moonlit darkness. He never stumbled, never faltered, making her wonder whether he could see in the darkness, like the predatory wolf he reminded her of. Then they emerged at the edge of the lake, and Alissa faltered to a halt at the sight before her.

The moon reflected off the ice, glinting on clumps of snow near the shore. The night was clear, the sky blue-black and dotted with stars. It should have been cold, but the trail ended in an alcove of sorts, where branches overlapped to form a curved, sheltered area, and outthrust roots offered a natural bench.

Intimacy and romance seemed to glow in the crisp air.

Startled by the fancy, and by Tucker's actions, Alissa turned to him. "This is lovely."

"I found it last year. Used to be a rendezvous point for drug trafficking." He stood back in the shadows, away from the warmth of the moonlight. "You seemed like you needed a moment. Parry said he'd put a cop outside your house, and I figured you'd want some privacy. Go ahead and cry if you need to. I don't mind. If you'd rather, I'll wait up the trail a bit."

But he wouldn't leave her completely alone, just in case. The knowledge should have made her feel trapped. Instead, it made her feel safer. Not completely safe, but more protected than if she were utterly alone, which was how she had been feeling in the car.

"No," she said. "Stay. I don't think I need to cry anymore." She tightened her parka around her body and sat on a tree root, facing out over the frozen water.

When she shivered, he sat next to her, close enough that she could feel his untamed warmth, close enough that she could have leaned if she'd wanted to. "I'm not afraid of waterworks," he said, staring out at the ice as though seeing something else. "My mother was big on tears."

He didn't sound irritated by the fact, as she might have expected. Instead he sounded sad.

Outside their little shelter, snow began to fall in big, fluffy flakes that coasted to gentle landings. The world was quickly frosted in white, the nighttime noises deadened beneath the winter weight, lending even more privacy to their retreat. The knowledge that the small space had once been home to drug dealers should have darkened its beauty. Instead, it lent a sharp edge to the moment, a feeling of quiet desperation that Alissa couldn't quite identify, couldn't quite deal with.

"Why did your mother cry?" she asked, knowing it was none of her business, but also knowing that he'd broken down one of the professional barriers between them when he'd turned off the road and brought her to this spot. Whatever it had been in the past, Tucker's familiarity with the path suggested that he had made it into his own space in the months since. A space for reflection, perhaps, or for the old grief that tinged his expression now.

"She hated to move," he said simply, "and we traveled a lot. My dad was in the military, and we never knew if it would be a few months or a couple of years before he'd get new orders. She hated it."

And Tucker had loved it, Alissa thought. Loved the newness of it, the never-ending change. He must have, or he wouldn't be living the life he was now, a new cop shop every few years, new scenery, new friends.

That was what she'd heard in his voice, the guilt that he'd loved travel when his mother hadn't. Guilt that he'd had no problem picking up and leaving. Or if not guilt, then regret, at the very least.

The realization was scant comfort, and irritation pushed the words out of Alissa's mouth before she could call them back. "Well, at least your father kept her around that long. Mine found a better family and took a hike with his other kids." Then she sucked in a breath on an embarrassed hiss. "I'm sorry. That was mean and irrelevant."

"Perhaps not so irrelevant as all that," Tucker said. He kept his focus on the lake, but reached over to take her hand. They had both stripped off their gloves in the SUV, and the touch of his bare fingers was a jolt of warmth her system didn't need, couldn't trust. "You're used to being left and I'm used to doing the leaving. Bad combination."

"No combination," she said flatly, but damned if her fingers didn't tangle with his and hang on tight. Damned if warmth didn't flutter to life in her chest, in her center, bringing memories of another night they'd shared. "We wouldn't be working together if it weren't for Chief Parry, and we wouldn't be here now if it wasn't for the bomb." *Bombs,* her mind supplied, reminding her of the danger, which suddenly seemed too close to the small, intimate space.

"We're working together because of Parry, true," Tucker agreed, "but he has nothing to do with us being *here*." He indicated the twining branches, the moonlit lake and the falling snow.

"Why *are* we here?" Alissa asked. She pulled her hand from his, torn between a sudden, inexplicable case of nerves and the burgeoning warmth that seemed intent on taking over her body, focused at the points where she and Tucker touched at hip and shoulder.

"Damned if I know." His voice roughened with frustration, or perhaps something more elemental. "Maybe because you looked like you needed a break. Maybe because I did." He sighed and stretched, and when he subsided, he'd slid one arm behind her in a move that might have seemed calculated if it hadn't been for his agitation. "I know we said we wouldn't let that night at the club turn into a thing, but I'm having trouble forgetting about it. When that tunnel blew…when you pulled that paper off your car…" He blew out a breath. "God, that scared the hell out of me."

His raw, brutal honesty pierced her like lightning

and battered down a few of her carefully constructed defenses. But still, she held the emotions away, knowing they were dangerous, and just as foolish as wishing her father home after all these years. "You would have been worried for any co-worker."

He turned to face her, and in the moonlight his dark eyes were darker still, his face shadowed, until it was difficult to tell where he ended and the night began. "Not this way. Not like this. I'm going crazy here, not because you're a cop, but because you're you."

And before she could react, if her suddenly paralyzed brain could have reacted at all, he leaned forward and touched his lips to hers. He left her plenty of room to ease back, to escape and not let this get any more complicated than it already was.

But it was already too late.

Chapter Five

Tucker imagined that somewhere a part of his brain was shouting for attention, telling him this was a damned dumb stunt to pull, telling him he'd been an idiot to bring her down by the water, a fool for thinking she'd needed comforting, a moron for thinking he should be the one to comfort her.

But he couldn't hear that part of his brain over the rushing, spinning roar of lust that overtook him the moment Alissa's lips softened, the moment her fingers tightened on his and her breath escaped on a throaty sigh of acquiescence.

Of temptation.

Kissing her was stupid, unprofessional, all the things he'd told himself as he'd walked away from her car that night at the club with a hard-on that wouldn't quit and a howl of desperation in his heart. But he couldn't make himself pull back now, couldn't hold himself back when her lips parted beneath his. Instead he crowded closer and demanded more, even though he knew he shouldn't.

He was the absolute wrong man for her. Learning of her father's desertion only confirmed what he'd known from the first. She was a nester. She wanted roots and promises. He wanted freedom.

But those problems were lost to reason when her tongue stroked greedily alongside his, when her hands dug into his leather jacket and held fast, bringing them closer, binding them together.

Instead of pulling away as he ought to do, he twisted toward her and slid his arms around her body, cradling her, anchoring her. She murmured agreement and shifted her grip, sliding her hands inside his suddenly too-hot jacket. She stroked her fingertips along his ribs and stomach, leaving trails of fire through layers of clothing.

Barely breaking contact, he shrugged out of his jacket, then swung her onto his lap so that she straddled him. Her knees gripped his hips, keeping their bodies torturously apart when he wanted. He didn't know what he wanted anymore, only that he wanted more of it. All of it.

He was vaguely aware of the snow falling more heavily outside their small nook, vaguely conscious of flakes filtering down to touch his cheek and hair, where they melted immediately to warm wetness. It wouldn't have surprised him if the snow had simply vaporized off his overheated skin. The fires of excitement burned hot and hotter still as Alissa framed his face in her hands and rose over him for a deep kiss that arrowed straight to his soul.

With a groan, or maybe a curse, he slid his hands up beneath her parka to her trim waist, and used this new grip to urge her closer to him, until her slender legs flanked him and her center chafed his aching fullness.

At that final touch, that ultimate apposition, she stiffened and pulled away from him, though she kept her hands on his face, her eyes near his. Her breathing was quick and harried, though he could barely hear it over the rattling of his own lungs, the roar of his blood. But her sudden stillness brought his eyes open. In the snow-brightened moonlight, he saw that her expression was shuttered.

Somehow the moment had been lost.

He fought for calmness, even as their labored breaths forced their bodies together and apart, together and apart, in a ghostly parody of the sexual act they had been racing toward, just as they had that night in her car.

Oh, hell, he thought, remembering that night. They'd been in nearly the same position, her atop him in the front seat, her legs around his waist, their tongues intertwined, when he'd knocked her badge off the console and started the whole downward spiral that led them away from mutual satisfaction and straight toward…

Right now.

He groaned aloud and her shoulders relaxed a notch. She scooted back, so she was closer to his knees than his lap and said, "I feel like we've played this scene before."

"Yeah," he grated. "Only, that time I was able to walk away. After today…" Hell, after the past few months, when she'd been close enough to touch, yet so distant. "After today I'm not walking."

"Perhaps not." Her back was to the moonlight, so she was little more than a mysterious shadow of dark against the falling snow. He couldn't see her expression, but her voice was an odd mix of wistful and tough when she said, "I guess it's my turn to pull back, then. Even if you're not walking now, you will soon enough."

There was a faint challenge in her words, along with that hint of wistfulness.

He nodded. "Yeah. My transfer went through. As soon as the kidnapper is caught—" and he was certain she was safe "—I'll be on my way to Rock Creek." He paused, half hoping for a shadow of regret, but found only the restlessness that had been plaguing him for the past few months, the itchiness that told him it was time to move on.

"Then I'll save you the bother of an awkward goodbye." She levered off his lap, leaving the warm spots to chill. "You're handsome enough and a darned good kisser, but I've been there, done that, bought the sweatshirt." Her shrug was silhouetted against the falling snow. "I'm better off alone than tangled up with someone who already has one foot out the door."

He rose and squared off opposite her, wanting to argue but knowing she was right. She'd just listed the very reasons he'd given himself for staying away. So why did he want to contradict her?

Stubbornness, he told himself, but he feared it was something else.

He wanted to pull her into his arms and kiss her until she was ready to throw away logic, just as he had been moments earlier. He wanted to run away from the temptation, give in to the rash restlessness that drove him from place to place, but that would only prove once and for all that he was his father's son, able to break a woman's heart simply by following his own.

So, he leaned down with studied nonchalance, grabbed his jacket from its resting place on the gnarled roots and shrugged into it, accepting the cold shock as nothing less than he deserved. Then he held out a hand. "Ready to head back to the truck?"

"Yeah." She shoved her hands in the pockets of her parka. "You lead. I think we'd be better off not touching each other. Less chance for temp—" she coughed to cover the word "—confusion. Less chance for confusion."

"You got it." But he was absurdly pleased at the cut-off word. Temptation. Yeah, that was it. *Temptation.* He was tempted by her lips, by her endless legs and by the steel that stiffened her delicate spine, even when things were going to hell around her.

But he couldn't afford to be tempted, for both of their sakes. He was leaving, and she deserved better in any event. He'd proven once before that he didn't know what to do with a good woman's heart.

Hell, he barely even knew what to do with his own.

But as they trudged back up the narrow path, leaving dark footprints in the virgin snow, he realized that he didn't regret bringing her down to his spot by the lake.

If nothing else, she had lost the devastated look she'd carried in her eyes when they left the station. And it had probably been for the best that they deal with their attraction and get it out in the open.

Part of him wished that they hadn't kissed again, that he hadn't been reminded of her potent, edgy flavor and the feel of her body against his. But the greater part of him couldn't regret the stolen moments.

"Look at it this way." He glanced back over his shoulder as they neared the top of the trail. "Now that we've got this settled, none of the other cops need to know about what happened between us. We can keep it professional until I leave."

"Good point," she agreed, though there was something flat in her tone. He would have stopped and asked her about it, but at that moment they emerged from the tree line and stepped into the parking area.

There was another vehicle parked alongside his SUV.

AHEAD OF ALISSA ON THE PATH, Tucker stiffened and muttered a low, vicious curse. Her heart jackrabbited, and she reached for her weapon even as she pushed to his side. "What is it?"

Then she stopped and swore at the sight that greeted her eyes. A plain sedan sat beside Tucker's SUV.

The magnetized bubble on its roof flashed with lights that should have been reassuring, but were anything but.

The car doors opened. Detectives Tracy Mendoza

and Russell Piedmont climbed out, faces set in identical grim lines.

"Damn it, McDermott," Piedmont snapped. He tugged his BCCPD ball cap down over his thinning brown hair. Temper cut grooves into his tanned face, which would have been handsome if he didn't always look one step away from ticked off. "I was just about to call—" His mouth snapped shut when he saw Alissa at Tucker's side. He snorted. "Oh."

Alissa blushed, and hated herself for it. *Way to look guilty, Wyatt.* Worse, Tucker stepped slightly ahead of her, shielding her with his body as though she needed protection from her own co-workers.

Then again, maybe he wasn't far wrong. Piedmont had already tried to convince Parry to disband the new Forensics Department and tempt Fitz back on the job, and Tracy Mendoza had been less than welcoming.

Now Mendoza narrowed her eyes and glanced to the pristine snow covering the parking lot, then back at Tucker. "You two were down there quite some time, weren't you?"

Though she had seemed to soften slightly at the earlier task force meeting, Mendoza's attitude was back in force now. Alissa felt a dull thud of disappointment and a low twist of shame. Denial was futile, because anything they said would be misinterpreted or downright ignored.

Besides, it would be a lie. They had been down by the water doing exactly what the other cops were thinking. They'd been hooking up. Necking like teenagers. Nearly making lo—having sex.

Any way Alissa looked at it, she'd made a mistake. A stupid, unprofessional mistake. But she had long ago learned that nobody else was going to save her, nobody else was going to blunt the sting of rejection, loneliness or bad calls. So she stepped out from behind Tucker and crossed her arms and said challengingly, "You have new information on the case?"

Mendoza smirked. "What? Like you two are on duty? Please."

Piedmont echoed her sneer, but said, "The chief asked us to do a drive-by of Wyatt's house. Imagine our surprise to see McDermott's ride in an abandoned parking lot with no footprints, no signs of life. We hiked up the main trail a bit, calling, but apparently you didn't hear us." The corners of his mouth tipped up further. "Must've been too busy."

"Did you call base?" Tucker asked as though he didn't care either way. His stance and expression suggested that he and Alissa had done nothing wrong, that he had nothing to hide, nothing to apologize for.

So why did she feel as if she needed to do all those things? Because, she realized with a hollow thud of disappointment, what had happened down by the lake had mattered more to her than it had to him. As usual.

"I was just about to radio it in," Piedmont answered curtly. "You got lucky."

Mendoza smirked at the double entendre.

"Well, as you can see, we're fine." Tucker waved them off. "Thanks for stopping in and checking. See you in the morning."

Alissa sensed that the cops wanted to say something more, that they would have if she'd been alone, or with someone less imposing than McDermott. Though he didn't have many years on the job in the BCCPD, she had noticed—and cursed herself for noticing—that he was accorded the respect of an old-timer, right up there alongside Fitz, right below the chief.

In the past, the unfairness of it had chafed. Right now she was glad for it, because Piedmont and Mendoza each gave her a last long look and returned to their vehicle. The engine started, but the sedan didn't pull out. Instead, the partners sat and waited. Watching.

Tucker gestured Alissa to the SUV and said, "Let's get the hell out of here."

She would have belted him if he'd held the door for her, and the lift of his eyebrow said he knew it full well. Once they were inside the SUV with the doors shut and the engine running, Piedmont backed up, then sped off, slaloming through the fresh snow.

Leaving Tucker and Alissa alone once again.

The awkward silence stretched thin while he pulled out of the parking area and onto the main road, which was slick with salt-melted snow. The windshield wipers moved with rhythmic swipes, counterpointing the hiss of tires on wet tarmac.

They both spoke at once, the same two words. "I'm sorry."

A bubble of sour amusement lodged in Alissa's throat, and she shot him a glance. "You first."

He chuckled, though it sounded forced, as though

he was making himself see humor in a humorless situation. "I'm sorry I pulled off in the parking area. I should've known Chief Parry would send someone after us. If I'd driven you straight home, none of that would have happened."

She wondered whether *that* included the kisses and confidences they'd shared in that small, intimate space, or whether he was speaking solely of their discovery by Piedmont and Mendoza, which smacked of high school embarrassments and the college walk of shame.

Then she realized she didn't want to know.

She sighed as they turned onto the final road near her home. "I think Chief Parry's strategy is about to backfire. Instead of me becoming more popular by association, I bet you're about to become part of the Forensic Department outcasts, along with me, Cassie and Maya. Sorry."

He shrugged as he pulled into her driveway. "Doesn't matter. I'm out of here in a few weeks, anyway. Sooner, if we can close this case." He parked and killed the engine, then turned to her. "They'd probably warm up to you pretty damn quick if we catch this guy."

He'd said *we*, but the plural didn't please her this time. He was being too careful to remind her that they were nothing more than temporary partners. She should do herself a favor and remember that.

So she lifted her chin. "The respect of my co-workers is the last thing I'm thinking about on this case. I want to catch this guy because he needs to be caught. Period."

There was no way she was letting another monster walk. Not on her watch.

But instead of approval or agreement, Tucker's expression showed reservations when he said, "I don't suppose I could talk you into taking a bit of a background role, right?" When she said nothing, merely looked at him, he sighed and let his head fall back against the headrest. "Didn't think so. Doesn't it matter that he's targeted you? That he's tried to kill you twice now?"

A chill worked its way through her gut, even through her heavy parka and the heated air in the vehicle. "Of course it matters," she snapped, annoyed with him, with herself. "But what do you want me to do? Quit? Not likely. The victims need me." As they had needed her before. She blew out a frustrated breath. "And, for the record, any one of us could have gone into the ice tunnel and been trapped."

"True," he agreed, "but it wasn't just anyone. It was you. And that car bomb was pretty damn specific."

This time she did shiver, and hated him for being right. "I know." She glanced at him. "But that doesn't mean I'm quitting."

They stared at each other as the interior light finally clicked off, leaving them in darkness broken only by her front light. On the street a car approached, then slowed.

Alissa stiffened, then grumbled when Piedmont's sedan cruised past with a cocky beep-beep. "Jerk."

"No arguments there. Come on, let's go inside." Tucker was out of the SUV before Alissa's brain fully processed his words.

She nearly leapt from the vehicle. "Oh, no. No, you

don't. You're not coming inside." *You're not staying here!*

But that was what the chief had said earlier, back when her blast-rattled brain had chosen to let the words slide. He'd said they should stick together. Watch each other's backs, with on-duty drive-bys at regular intervals. It made logical sense, as they'd been the only cops to receive notes.

But the chief had no idea that when Alissa was alone with Tucker, logic had a way of leaping right out the window.

Damn it, this was *not* going to be good.

She followed him to her door, ready for battle. "You're not staying here."

He stood aside and let her unlock the door, didn't argue when she blocked the opening with her body, as though 120 pounds of her could defeat his two hundred of solid muscle. He stood too close, reminding her of his warmth and his scent, giving her a close-up view of the lighter glints in his dark-brown eyes.

She expected him to argue, or push past her. Instead he inclined his head so his longish dark hair brushed against the collar of his leather jacket, and said, "I'm either sleeping on your sofa or in the SUV. Your call, but I'd really prefer the couch."

When he said it that way, so rationally and completely lacking in sexual innuendo, it made her feel foolish, as though she was the only one doubting her own willpower.

They were professionals. Partners, if only for a short

while. Hell, she'd been partners with a guy before, and they'd managed to make it work. She and her partner in Tecumseh had pulled surveillance together, crashed at each other's places. It hadn't been an issue.

Except that she'd tolerated Butch rather than liking him. She hadn't approved of his cowboy ways and his disrespect for protocol. And in the end it had bitten them both in the ass.

How could she protect herself from making another mistake like that? How could she be sure of controlling the uncontrollable Tucker McDermott?

Heck, how could she be sure of controlling herself?

She couldn't, she realized. And that was what scared her the most.

In the distance she saw headlights approach, then pause. The sedan cruised by a second time, this time beeping once in a mocking blast.

That decided her. She stepped back and waved him inside. "Fine. You can have the couch."

Once he was inside, she shut and locked the door. He prowled ahead of her, checking windows and rooms for signs of any disturbance. If she'd been alone, she would have done the same. Because he'd beaten her to it, making her feel as though he considered her weak and helpless, she set her teeth and headed for the kitchen.

The food options were pretty lame, since the case had consumed all of her time over the past two weeks. She took stock and tried to make the best of it.

"All clear," Tucker said from behind her.

She jumped, startled, then cursed herself for the

quick jangle of nerves. She turned toward him and forced herself not to retreat a step, not to let him see how much his presence affected her. Or maybe it wasn't entirely him. Maybe part of it was the sudden sense of the night pressing in from the dark windows. The snow had stopped, leaving the outer world colder and more menacing than it had seemed before. Leaving her confused by the war of hot and cold within her.

She gestured toward the refrigerator. "There's food. Take whatever."

He seemed to sense her confusion, or maybe it resonated with him at some level. He reached out and touched her cheek, leaving a fine sizzle of want where his fingers rested. "Get some rest. Tomorrow is another day, another chance to break this case wide open. Until then, there's safety in numbers. Chief'll have cars cruising past every half hour or so, and anyone who wants you will have to get through me first. I'm a light sleeper." Instead of reassuring her, that last detail brought a prickle of nerves and heat to the surface of her skin. His eyes darkened and his voice dropped a notch when he said, "As for the other…don't worry. You made yourself clear down by the lake, and we both know you're right." He grinned suddenly. "Not particularly daring, but right."

She laughed, and just like that, the tension between them relaxed a notch. Attraction admitted to and dismissed.

Or at least tempered for the moment.

"Fine, call me a wimp." She stretched and faked a

yawn. "I'm going to bed. Pillows and blankets are in the hall closet. Wake me if things get interesting."

The corners of his sensual mouth turned up. "Define *interesting*."

"You know, bullets and bombs, that sort of thing." She'd meant it to sound playful, but it came out sarcastic. She grimaced. "Sorry—I can't help thinking about the other girls."

The memory of Lizzie's brutal tears tore at her heart, reminding her that this had been more than another day on the job.

"I know." Tucker's dark eyes reflected his own worry. "But you can't be on duty 24/7. So shut it off for a few hours. I'll be here when you wake up."

The promise shouldn't have been tempting, shouldn't have been soothing, but once she'd changed, brushed her teeth and slipped between the sheets in the master bedroom, she found the rigid set of her shoulders easing, found sleep coming more quickly than she'd expected. She should have been a bundle of nervous energy, knowing that she'd been targeted by a kidnapper's rage, and that super-sexy Tucker McDermott was a thin door panel away.

Instead she slept like the dead.

THE STRIDENT RING of the telephone knocked Alissa to full consciousness. She lurched up in bed, grabbed for the phone and found only empty air. The handset wasn't in its cradle.

"Damn it!" Her head spun, and every square inch of

her body ached like fury, instantly reminding her of the events of the previous day.

She swore and struggled to her feet when the phone rang again.

It was full light, and the too-bright winter sun slashing through her curtained bedroom window told her it was well into morning. The phone mercifully quit ringing as she hauled a sweatshirt on over the stretchy pants and t-shirt she'd slept in. She jammed a ball cap on her frizzy hair and muttered, "I'm up already."

The clock said 9:10, but her head hadn't hit the pillow until nearly 2:00 that morning, leaving her tired and irritable. Or maybe it was the knowledge that she'd have to face Tucker first thing, wearing her fuzzy socks and a nasty case of bed-head.

But there was no way in hell she was primping before coffee, so she pushed open her bedroom door—

And stopped dead at the sight of Tucker, standing beside her couch bare-chested, talking on her phone. Their eyes met, and she forced herself to return his gaze rather than letting her eyes feast on the sight of his broadly muscled shoulders and the fine swirls of hair that accented his physique. His pecs stood out against the wall of his chest, defined with smooth skin but little body fat. His abs were a ripple of muscle, and the flatness near his navel drew her eyes downward to—

It wasn't until he muttered an oath and reached down to drag his shirt over his shoulders that she realized she hadn't managed to keep her eyes on his, after all. She'd been ogling.

And damn, it had been good.

"For you," he said flatly, holding out the phone. "Your boyfriend."

What the heck? Confused, she took the receiver. "Hello?"

"Alissa! Thank God you're okay."

"Aiden?" She turned away from Tucker, who was scowling as he buttoned his shirt. "What's the matter? What do you need?"

She knew he wouldn't have called if it hadn't been in his best interest, and had no clue why he would have told Tucker he was her boyfriend when they'd been split up for months.

"I wanted to make sure you'd heard," he said in the dramatic anchorman's voice he'd worked so hard to perfect. "But I can see the Tecumseh PD beat me to it, if you've already got security on the premises."

"Heard what?" she parroted dumbly, mind racing. What did Aiden know that she didn't? Had he heard about the attempts on her life? Granted, he was in a national newsroom now, but the BCCPD and the FBI had been careful to downplay the abductions, lest the media play into the kidnapper's hands.

"About Johnny Ferguson, of course." Aiden's voice warmed. "You mean you *haven't* heard? I'm surprised nobody called you."

"Tell me," she said numbly, as a horrible, unbelievable possibility occurred to her. She was aware of Tucker's attention sharpening, aware of him crossing to her side and leaning in to listen when Aiden's voice spoke in her ear.

"Ferguson broke probation two weeks ago and grabbed a teenager outside a Tecumseh movie theater. She got away and he hasn't been seen since. He was spotted last night, about ten miles south of Bear Claw." Aiden's voice held an odd combination of concern and glee when he asked, "Remember what he said when he found out in court that you'd been the one to give his name to the Denver cops?"

She shivered against sudden cold and let her eyes meet Tucker's when she said, "Yeah. I remember." Then she parroted back the words that had been engraved on her brain two years earlier. "He said, 'When I get out, bitch, I'm coming after you.'"

What if he had?

Chapter Six

Tucker barely restrained himself from grabbing the handset and shouting into the phone, demanding more information about a probation jumper named Ferguson, about the man on the other end of the phone, who'd identified himself as Alissa's boyfriend, yet now seemed intent on pumping her for information.

Her shoulders stiffened another degree, until they were so tight he thought she might snap into a thousand pieces if he touched her. Her voice cooled when she said, "No, Aiden, I will not give you an interview about Ferguson or the new case....No, not even to help your career." She sighed and tugged on the brim of her ball cap, which covered a mass of honey-blond waves.

Apparently, Officer Wyatt's hair frizzed overnight. Tucker knew he shouldn't find that detail endearing, but like her vulnerability the night before, when she'd cried and he'd taken her to his spot down by the lake, this new chink in her brittle, professional armor drew him in unexpected ways.

In unwise ways, he told himself. She wasn't the sort of woman a man should love and leave, even if the ground rules were clearly spelled out at the beginning. He'd tried that once before, with a dispatcher three, maybe four cities ago.

Pretty Helen had been divorced for two years, had no kids—he was careful not to mess with the kid thing—and was looking for a good time. She'd claimed to be relieved that he didn't want anything serious. And maybe she had been at first. But somewhere along the line she'd gotten involved, and he hadn't seen it in time.

He blamed himself for that, and for not handling it better when she'd asked him to stay.

"I'm hanging up now, Aiden." Alissa's chilly tones snapped him out of the uncomfortable memories. Her face was pale and drawn. "You'll have to get that promotion on your own merit…or not." She made a face as she clicked the phone off.

"Problem?" Tucker asked.

"Ex-boyfriend," she said succinctly, "trying to make the leap from sports desk to anchor, and thinking that I might be his ticket." She glanced at Tucker, and he saw the fear behind her dry facade. "There was a rape case back in Tecumseh. We got the guy, but he wiggled free and then got himself convicted elsewhere. Seems like he's out again."

She stood there in the middle of her determinedly cheerful living room, looking lost and alone and nearly swallowed up by an oversize sweatshirt. With her slim legs clad only in a clingy layer of material and her hair stuffed up under a cap, she looked too small, too young, too breakable. Tucker wanted to fold her into his arms and promise to protect her, promise to chase those shadows out of her eyes.

Instead, he jerked his head toward the bedroom. "Get dressed. You can tell me about it while we're driving."

They needed to report in fast. Based on what he'd overheard, this Ferguson could be their bomber.

Hell, he could even be their kidnapper. It wasn't much of a jump from serial rapist to kidnapper, especially when the victims were teenage girls.

Once they were buckled into the SUV and on their way to the station, he glanced over at Alissa and raised an eyebrow in silent inquiry.

She rubbed her narrow hands across her face. "Two freshmen were grabbed, driven off site, raped and returned to campus. They were blindfolded and traumatized, and it was…" She paused, swallowed and said, "Ugly."

That simple word, he knew, encompassed days and weeks, maybe months of wading through leads that went nowhere. It covered the hopeless, ravaged faces of the victims and the tricky mental blockades borne of guilt and shame. The word held empathy and anger, determination and failure.

He knew, because he'd been on similar cases. He'd felt all those things. And he imagined that sexist though it might sound, cases like that were probably harder on a female cop.

He turned a corner, waved at the two junior

officers that had watched Alissa's house overnight and said, "You don't have to tell me if you don't want."

"I might as well," she said, her voice rough with emotion. "The Tecumseh PD formed a task force to solve the rapes. The public was screaming for justice, the politicians for an arrest. We finally got a solid tip on the hotline, someone claiming it was this neighbor of theirs, a punk kid named Ferguson who'd been in and out of the foster system and had a bad history with women. We checked it out, built our case, made the arrest." She grimaced at the unpleasant memory. "My partner skipped a step and Ferguson's lawyer was an underpaid up-and-comer looking to change jobs. He argued his butt off and got key evidence excluded. The judge didn't want to, but he had to dismiss."

"Ouch." Tucker winced. "That explains a lot." Like why mentions of instinct and gut feeling made her testy when most artists he knew had softer, more easygoing natures.

"Not even close," she said bluntly. "Eighteen months later, there was another string of rapes in a city to the north. I got suspicious—just hadn't been able to get Ferguson's ratty face out of my mind—and collaborated with the PD up there to reel him in. When they brought him in, I…I had to be there. He saw me and knew."

Tucker's stomach soured, and he bypassed his usual takeout-coffee drive-thru. "Thus, the threat." Her earlier words echoed in his brain, where they'd been engraved by the impotent anger in her voice.

When I get out, bitch, I'm coming after you.

A surge of protectiveness rocked Tucker as he pulled into the station parking lot. The sad remains of Alissa's VW had been removed, presumably to the bomb squad garage. The burned, blackened marks had been covered over by fresh snow and then plowed and salted into oblivion. But his mind's eye showed him the scene as it had been, and his gut tightened on the memory.

Scowling, he parked the SUV as close to the door as he could get it. "Wait for me. I'll let you out."

She didn't wait, of course, which left him scrambling to cover her as she stalked to the door, visibly annoyed. But when he caught up and hustled her into the relative safety of the station house, he saw that it wasn't annoyance in her eyes.

It was fear.

The realization was a blow to his gut, and before he could stop himself, he said, "I won't let him get to you. I promise."

Her eyes flashed to his, holding surprise and maybe a hint of resentment. But instead of the denial he expected, she inclined her head. "I hate it, but I may have to take you up on that." Then she sucked in a breath and squared her shoulders. "Come on, let's tell Chief Parry and get the wheels turning."

She strode down the hall alone, radiating the no-nonsense competence that she wore like a shield. In that moment Tucker realized that the attitude didn't fly for him, because over the past twenty-four hours, he'd seen past the cop to the woman beneath.

And damned if he didn't like her.

ALISSA HELD IT together through the briefing by sheer force of will, but it was a struggle. Where the night before the room had warmed to her and the officers' expressions hadn't seemed so angry, now she was back to being an outcast. When she finished her report, she could see it in their faces, that look of *You brought him here. This is your fault.*

But she couldn't blame them. The more she thought about it, the more Chief Parry and the others asked for clarification, the more she started to believe that Ferguson had come after her.

As though she'd said it aloud, a sea of grumbles rose up from the assembled cops, barely slackening when Maya raised her hand. Chief Parry acknowledged her, and she rose to stand at the front of the room.

She glared out at the assembled cops. "Okay, people, you've had your moment. Now let's think about this rationally." She looked toward where Alissa and Cassie sat shoulder to shoulder. "As I would have told Wyatt if she'd come to me first—" she left the admonition hanging long enough to make Alissa feel even worse "—it's not a perfect fit."

"Begging your pardon, Doc," Mendoza said, emphasizing the title so it sounded like an insult, "but Ferguson fits your profile. He's white, male, in his thirties and has social issues."

"That also describes sixty percent of the people in this room," Maya said tartly, surprising a snicker out of Alissa.

She heard it echo behind her and turned to find Tucker two rows back, surrounded by empty chairs on all sides as though he, too, was an island amidst the task force. It shamed her to know that he'd been shunned because of her, because of what Mendoza and Piedmont had thought they'd seen. Or maybe, she thought as their eyes locked across the short distance and electricity arced straight to her soul, the others stayed away because of his dark, dangerous air and the sense of wildness, which was heightened as though he was a predator on alert.

Or a protector on the job.

His earlier promise shouldn't have made her feel safer. She was better off depending on herself, and on Cassie and Maya, who had proven themselves loyal. She shouldn't depend on a cop like Tucker, who was already halfway gone. But because his promise of protection had made her feel better, because she was too aware of him sitting two rows away, she turned, faced forward and told herself to ignore him.

Told herself to focus on the job.

"Johnny Ferguson does fit some of the traits, but there are a few gaps," Maya said. "For one, Lizzie wasn't sexually assaulted. For another, if his goal was revenge against Alissa, then why address yesterday's letter to Detective McDermott? It was sheer chance that Alissa found the tunnel. If he'd been targeting her, he'd have been more direct."

"The car bomb seemed pretty damned direct to me," Piedmont said. "Maybe he was working up to it."

"Or maybe we don't know the full story yet. Heck, we don't even know if Ferguson has explosives knowledge," Maya returned. She drew breath to say something more to the shifting crowd, but Parry held up a hand.

"Thank you, Dr. Cooper. That'll do." When she returned to her seat beside Alissa, he addressed the task force. "You heard her, people. It's a lead, but not the only one." With that, he handed out the day's assignments. Maya was instructed to speak with Lizzie again, both to help the girl and to probe for any additional information.

The chief then turned to Cassie. "I want you to pick up the FBI evidence specialist at noon. Show him around. Get his take on things." He turned to Alissa before Cassie's sneer could form. "And Wyatt—"

"I know," she interrupted. "I'll get to work on tracking down Ferguson. I can get in touch with the officers who pulled him in on the last set of rapes, then I'll talk to his parole officer."

"Give their names to Piedmont. I'm keeping you off Ferguson."

It took a moment for the chief's words to penetrate. Then Alissa shot to her feet. "What? You can't be—" she stopped herself and ended with a plaintive "—sir?"

Had she done something to make him think she couldn't handle the work?

"Stand down, Wyatt," the chief said, not unkindly. "Teamwork, remember? I need you to work on the skull you uncovered yesterday. The ME's done with his first look, and we can send the rest to a specialist if necessary, but I'd like you do a full reconstruction. Computer, clay, whatever you think is best. That's why I hired you."

Intentional or not, his words were a subtle dig that she had yet to fully show off her skills as an artist or a reconstructor. So she nodded. "I'll have something for you by the end of the day."

And she'd make time to check into the whereabouts of Johnny Ferguson, as well. If Aiden's information was correct, Ferguson had broken parole a few days before the first kidnapping.

Coincidence or cause and effect?

She didn't know, but she was damn sure going to find out. It wasn't that she didn't trust Mendoza and Piedmont to do a good job, but…okay, she didn't trust them. Not after the night before. And besides, she was used to relying on herself.

Parry moved on to the others. "McDermott, I'm putting you on Bradford Croft. I know his alibis checked out for the second and third kidnappings and Lizzie didn't ID him, but I want to know where he was all day yesterday. He gives me a weird vibe."

Croft lived next door to the Walsh family and had a prior sexual offense—a minor one, but minor offenses had a way of escalating to major ones over time. He'd seemed like a solid suspect, but the evidence just hadn't supported it. Not yet, anyway.

Tucker shifted in his chair. "With all due respect, sir, I'd prefer to work in the station today."

The room stilled except for Piedmont's snort.

Alissa's face flamed. Tucker couldn't have been any more obvious if he'd held her hand as they'd walked into the room. No doubt the rumor mill had already circulated Piedmont's version of the scene down by the lake, leaving little doubt as to the state of Alissa and Tucker's partnership. But when she glanced back at him, she saw that he didn't care. His jaw was set, his expression closed.

She supposed that made sense, really. It didn't matter whether the other cops liked him or not, because he was leaving. She would be the one staying behind. Again.

Ignoring a faint burn at the thought, she faced forward, expecting the chief to slap Tucker down.

Parry nodded. "Understandable, but I need you in the field. Watch your back, and don't forget that the first note was addressed to you."

The chief shut the meeting down soon after that, and Alissa stood and filed out with the others, feeling faintly depressed when Tucker walked off without a backward glance. No, she told herself, she wasn't depressed over him. She was tired of a job that was proving less specialized than she'd hoped, tired of co-workers who wouldn't cut her a break. Most of all, she was physically tired, dragging from the aches and bruises of the day before, though they could have been so much worse.

Needing a moment alone to regroup, she walked to the far end of the hall and jogged down the stairs to the gloomy space they'd been given to house the Forensics Department.

The gray walls and lack of windows cast a pall on the area, but she was grateful for the square footage. The beat cops and detectives upstairs made do with cubes and desks, with the occasional office for senior staff. The Forensics Department had three interconnecting rooms that housed the high-tech equipment they'd purchased with a grant that had helped convince Parry to hire them.

Maya and Alissa had staked out a corner of the smallest room for their equipment. Alissa's desk was wedged between a pair of gun lockers the BCCPD used for storage of spare weapons. Man-size and blastproof, the cabinets were empty now and just taking up space. Maintenance kept promising to move them, but Alissa would believe that when she saw it.

A big, square box sat on the corner of her cluttered desk, sealed with evidence tape.

The unidentified skull.

She thumped down beside the box, the excitement of having a reconstruction project dulled by disappointment and stress. She was unspeakably weary all of a sudden, unspeakably fed up with the BCCPD cops and their resentments.

She'd gone into law enforcement because of the things she'd grown up seeing, from landlords trying to extort sexual favors in lieu of rent, to back alley brawls in the hard city areas they'd frequented those first few years. Eventually her mother had accepted that her husband wasn't coming back, wasn't sending money. She'd gotten a job, then training, then a better job. Alissa had been left to fend for herself more often than not, but she'd been used to it by then. Used to the shouts outside on the city streets after midnight, the rising wail of sirens. It was the sirens that had hooked her, or rather the way the streets would grow quiet in their wake, the way the world seemed to take a big sigh of relief when the cops came.

But now…where was *her* sigh of relief? Where was the quiet moment she'd promised herself when her application to the BCCPD was accepted?

Where was the feeling of coming home?

"Hey," Tucker's voice said from behind her, "you okay?"

She jolted but didn't turn, hating that he'd caught her at weak moments two days running. Rubbing the heels of her hands across her dry eyes she said, "Don't you have a suspect to track?"

"I wanted to check on you first."

Warmth nudged at her heart alongside confusion. Irritation. She turned in her chair and stood, unwilling to let his large bulk loom over her, even from half a room away. He stood near the door, balanced on the balls of his feet as though ready to fight—or maybe run—at a moment's notice. His too-long hair brushed his shoulders in dark, untamed waves, and his near-black eyes pierced her with questions that she couldn't begin to interpret, much less answer.

A fine current of electricity buzzed through her at the tension in his body, the gleam in his eyes. But even as the heat rose in the air between them, she rejected the temptation, knowing that no good could come of the attraction.

She crossed her arms. "Why would you need to check on me? I'm a cop, Tucker. I can take care of myself." She shoved aside the memory of earlier that morning, where she'd nearly clung to him for reassurance. She was tough. She could stand on her own. She had to stand on her own, because she couldn't trust him to stand beside her.

"You heard Parry," he countered, taking a step inside the door that brought him only a few feet closer to her but raised the air temperature by too many degrees. "We're supposed to watch each other's backs. There's a good chance Ferguson is going to come after you, and I don't intend to let that happen."

His eyes bore into hers. It was a heady sensation to have all that restless, wild energy focused solely on her....

She lifted her chin and fought the urge to step back. "I appreciate the thought, but I'm fine. I'm a cop in a police station. I don't need to be babysat, so why don't you go do your thing and I'll do mine."

His body stilled. His eyes narrowed. "What are you saying?"

She uncrossed her arms and abandoned all pretense of coolness. "I'm saying that you're confusing the hell out of me. We've agreed that there's a certain level of…" She paused, searching for something less incendiary than the words that sprang to mind, like *lust, need* and *spontaneous combustion,* then continued "There's a certain physical attraction between us, but we've agreed that nothing's going to come of it. Yet here you are, rip-snorting around and acting all possessive. You can't have it both ways. Either we're partners for the duration of this case and you back off to normal partner distance, or else we're—" again, she searched for the right words, this time for a phrase more neutral than *on the fast track to becoming lovers,* "—involved."

She expected an argument, or maybe an explosion of the pent-up energy she could see vibrating through his strong frame. She braced herself for a shout, or even a kiss.

Instead, he crossed the room and dropped into Maya's desk chair, frustration and discomfort radiating off him in waves. He scrubbed a hand across his suddenly tired-looking face, and glanced up at her, eyes dark with an emotion she couldn't quite define. "I tried the relationship thing once. I was no good at it."

Of all the things she might have expected him to say, this wasn't even close. She sank into her own chair, aware of the space separating them from each other, of the office door separating them from the rest of the world. "That wasn't really what I was getting at."

But it seemed to be what he wanted to say. He clasped his hands loosely between his knees and said simply, "I tried to be content. She was everything I should have wanted—smart, beautiful, funny, generous…" He fell silent for a moment, then shrugged. "But I couldn't make it work, couldn't make the restlessness go away. She cried when I left." He glanced at Alissa, his eyes dark with regrets, not heartbreak. "I promised myself I'd never put another woman in that position. I'm…" Now it was his turn to search for the right word. Finally he sighed and said, "I don't do 'involved.'"

"I wasn't asking you to," Alissa said flatly, and cursed when she realized that maybe a small part of her had been asking just that. Damn it, she knew better than to mistake sexual attraction for love, to confuse heat with affection.

At least, she ought to know better by now.

"Then what are you asking?"

She sighed and stood, knowing that the same ingrained manners that prompted him to hold doors would send him to his feet, as well. When he rose, she crossed the room and opened the door to the hall. With the basement reserved for the Forensics Department, there was no foot traffic to disrupt their privacy, but her message was clear.

Hit the road, buddy.

But still he stood, waiting for her answer. When the silence grew awkward, she dropped her hand from the doorknob and leaned back against the wall, wishing things could be easier somehow.

She'd moved to Bear Claw City hoping to find her place among her friends and her new co-workers. She'd even hoped to meet someone, a firmly rooted man who would give her love and family. But so far nothing had gone as she'd hoped, and now her plans and her safety were being jeopardized by two men who couldn't be more different if they tried.

Johnny Ferguson and Tucker McDermott. One

wanted to hurt her and the other wanted anything but. Yet, at that moment, she felt in more danger from Tucker than from the kidnapper. Maybe it was being inside the safe-seeming walls of the PD. Maybe it was the tension that arced between them as he stood too close, until she could feel his warmth on her skin, sense his edgy restlessness on the air.

"I'm asking you to give me space." Alissa didn't look away, didn't try to fight the warmth spreading through her body, because she knew it would be a lost cause. But right now her body and mind were at cross purposes, and that wouldn't help the case or the victims. "I appreciate your honesty, but there's no way I'm getting involved with another guy who's just passing through. And since we can't seem to work together without it being an issue…" She left the statement hanging, and a perverse part of her hoped he would argue. When he didn't, she pushed away from the wall, until she was standing in the shadow cast by his big, backlit body. "Just go do your thing, okay, McDermott? I'll be safe here. Ferguson isn't going to come waltzing past a dozen or more cops."

"Yet he waltzed into the police station parking lot and managed to avoid all the surveillance cameras while wiring your VW," Tucker said, his words a warm breath across her face.

"I'll be fine," she maintained, though the hall outside suddenly seemed darker than ever. "Go be a detective and track down Bradford Croft. You work alone, remember?"

"Yeah," he said with grim finality. "I remember."

His eyes darkened, as though he was drawing a new barrier between them. "I'm sorry."

And she knew he wasn't simply apologizing for having interrupted her, or for complicating things the night before. He was apologizing for himself, for not being able to give her what she needed.

Hell, she told herself for the hundredth time, *at least he's honest about it.*

But somehow that was scant comfort when he turned away and left, his larger-than-life presence fading with each departing footfall, until she was alone in the office with little more company than a naked skull in a cardboard box.

She grimaced and returned to her desk, knowing it had to be this way. She opened the cardboard box, pulled on a pair of nonpowdered latex gloves and lifted the skull from its packing material.

She held it at eye level, pushing aside all the Yorick references she'd heard too many times during her reconstruction training, and tried to focus on the work. The ME's report said the skeleton had belonged to a white female around twenty years old. In that, at least, she fit the profile of the kidnapped girls, though her bones had been buried upwards of a decade earlier.

That detail nagged at Alissa, reminding her that Johnny Ferguson would have been barely a teenager back then, and living hundreds of miles away. But as she set to work loading the skull into the machine that would take sectional and cross-sectional scans of the bones and render a detailed three-dimensional computer version, something else nagged at her, as well. The first note hadn't had anything to do with her. It had been aimed at Tucker.

That argued against it being Ferguson.

Chapter Seven

Tucker told himself he shouldn't be annoyed by the scene in Alissa's office. She was right—it wasn't his job to protect her. There was a whole damn building worth of cops between her and the street, and whether or not they liked her personally, they weren't going to let a criminal grab her from the basement of the damn police station.

Still, something twisted in his gut as he pulled to a stop in front of the Walsh home. Alissa would have called it instinct and dismissed it, but Tucker knew better than to ignore his gut feeling. So he scanned the immediate area, knowing something had tripped his internal alarms.

The subdivision where the first victim lived was five, maybe ten years old. The houses were all cut from the same mold, but they varied with a different entryway here, an added room there. The burlap-wrapped landscaping looked neat, and the driveways and stone walks were all shoveled and salted. Nothing seemed out of place.

Senses sharp, Tucker pulled into the next-door driveway and rolled to the house where Bradford Croft lived with his mother. He felt a prickle along the back of his neck, a sense of watching eyes as he strode to the front door. His first response was to check the weapon nestled in its holster beneath his arm. The second was relief that Alissa was safe back at the station house.

He knocked, and the front door immediately swung inward. Tucker's brain clicked to detective mode at the sight of the man on the other side.

Croft was in his midtwenties, white and physically fit. He fit Maya's profile, sketchy though it was. He also lived with his fifty-six-year-old mother and had worked full-time at a local megamart ever since the bankruptcy of the video store he'd managed since high school. He had a community college degree in business, a prior for indecent exposure and alibis for two of the kidnapping time frames.

But something about him set off Tucker's warning bells.

Maybe it was the momentary irritation that shone in Bradford Croft's hazel eyes, or the stiff precision of his military buzz-cut hair when he'd never been in the military. Maybe it was the skull and crossbones inked across the back of Croft's left hand, or the fact that when his eyes met Tucker's, they quickly slid away.

Or maybe it was simply instinct.

"Detective," Croft said evenly, "what can I do for you?" He didn't step away from the door, didn't invite Tucker into the living room, which he knew from a previous visit resembled a Victorian spinster's parlor, all stiff-backed chairs, doilies and bric-a-brac that looked like it had been there for decades, though Esmerelda Croft had bought the place only three years earlier.

"Lizzie was found over in the state park yesterday," Tucker said, judging the man, judging his reaction.

"Yeah, I saw the news bulletin." Croft grinned, but somehow the expression didn't reach his eyes, which remained flat. Disconnected. "Reggie and Sandra must be thrilled!"

"I'm sure they are." Tucker angled his body so he could see past Croft, and faked a shiver, though he was plenty warm inside his lined leather jacket. "It's chilly out here. Mind if I come in? I just have a few follow-up questions for you."

"Um…" Croft shifted back in the doorway and glanced over his shoulder. "It's really not a good time. Mom's lying down and I'm on my way to work."

Tucker had read the reports. Esmerelda had been "indisposed" during two other follow-up visits, as well.

Suspicions aligned in his head, in his gut. What if Esmerelda was more than "lying down"? What if Croft had cleared the house out so he could use it to imprison the girls? Hell, it even made sense—he'd transported Lizzie to the state park so she'd think she had been far away. Lizzie's mention of a wooden shed didn't fit right away, unless he had set it up in his basement to keep the girls separated…

Tucker thought fast as adrenaline buzzed in his blood. Warrant or no warrant? His instincts told him to shove his way into the house and deal with the consequences later. But Alissa's story from Tecumseh had stuck with him, along with a couple of near misses of his own making when it came to having evidence thrown out in court.

As much as he wanted to save the girls and get the bastard, it did them no good if the kidnapper walked on some bogus lawyer-speak argument. So he eased back and said, "Then I'll make this quick." And be back in an hour with a warrant and backup. "Just a routine follow-up. Where were you yesterday morning between six and nine?"

The doctor thought that was the timing of Lizzie's dump, based on her body temperature at the time of rescue, and the ambient air temp, corrected for the fact that she'd been in a sheltered cave lined with ice and snow.

"Where was I?" Croft's face darkened and he opened the door wider, so it framed his shoulders. "I can't believe you people! How many times do I need to alibi myself?"

"Apparently at least once more," Tucker said, "and while you're at it, you can add last night to your list. Say between four and eight-thirty?"

The car bomb could have been planted any time after Alissa had parked it for the task force meeting, but the best guess was after dark, once the shift-change traffic had ebbed and the streets had quieted a degree.

"For the love of—" Croft leaned forward with a fierce scowl and hissed, "The little bitch lied. I never waggled my weenie at her. That whole sexual predator thing is bull. I got into a beef with her father over a job, and that was how he got me back. Understand?"

Tucker crowded into the doorway and got in Croft's glowering face. "You already lost that court battle. The jury thought you were slime, just like I do. You sure you want to take another shot at a trial?"

Urgency hummed through Tucker's veins, a sense that answers were at his fingertips, an absolute, utter conviction that he was on the verge of a breakthrough. And if that made him one of Alissa's "cowboys," then so be it. He knew his job, and he trusted his instincts.

Croft's face twisted and he lunged away from the door frame, out onto the porch. He grabbed Tucker's jacket and raised a fist.

Tucker didn't struggle, figuring that dragging the guy in for assaulting an officer was just as good as anything. He braced himself for the blow—

And a reedy voice interrupted from the doorway. "Bradford? Bradford! What on earth do you think you're doing?"

Croft let go of Tucker and spun as though scalded. "Ma! I thought you were sleeping!"

Shock ripped through Tucker's gut. Part of him had been sure Croft had done the mother. He kept his weight on the balls of his feet and his gun in its holster and carefully examined Esmerelda Croft. She was a tall, whip-thin woman whose tight skin and dark hair had fought a losing battle against the tide of time. Her eyes were sharp on her son, and deep lines grooved the corners of her mouth, more from scowls than cigarettes.

She transferred her glare to Tucker. "What do you want?"

He inclined his head. "Detective McDermott, ma'am. I need to know your son's whereabouts yesterday, and I'd like to take a look around your home, if you don't mind."

She snapped, "Yes, I mind, but I don't suppose that concerns you." She stepped back and waved them inside. "Bradford was home with me all day. I'll testify to it in court, if needs be."

Of course she would, Tucker thought. He hung back and let Croft precede him into the house. As Bradford passed his mother, she slapped him on the back of the head and spat something in an unfamiliar language. Italian, probably, which would fit with her dark hair and the faint sense of Old World in the decor.

He wasn't yet sure what else it fit with. Senses buzzing, he nodded to the far side of the living room, where a hallway led to the kitchen and to the stairs beyond. "Let's start in the basement. You go first."

Alone, that was the only way he could control the suspects and be sure neither of them would rabbit, but he wasn't sure enough to call in backup. Not yet.

"Bulb's out," Esmerelda said, challenging him with a stare. "I'll have to get a flashlight and a new bulb."

He nodded tightly. "Do it."

The flashlight was small, the yellow beam anemic as Bradford led the way through a door off the kitchen, down a solid flight of stairs to the basement. Esmerelda was next in line, followed by Tucker, whose very skin prickled with alertness. He stayed near the top of the stairs, near the light and the door, lest one of them thought about rushing him and taking him down.

But there was no rush, no violence. Croft cursed when the old bulb proved stubborn, but he had it changed out within moments. "Okay, all set. Hit the switch near the door."

Tucker did so, and braced himself to see—

Nothing. The bare bulb gleamed down on stacked boxes and dusty mountain bikes, on a trio of toolboxes and a furnace that chose that moment to kick on with an asthmatic rattle. No girls, no prefab sheds, nothing.

The sense of expectancy dampened a notch, but the feeling of urgency didn't dim.

"Over there, into the corner." Tucker gestured Esmerelda and Bradford away from the stairs. He checked the shadowy steps leading to an outside bulkhead, and glanced inside a freestanding wardrobe made of rusted steel. Empty.

Then he asked them to show him the rest of the house, and though he got a full array of grumbles and glowers from Bradford, Esmerelda merely snapped something in that foreign language and took him around.

Still nothing.

They looked into the attic and the garage, and the feeling of "gotcha" in Tucker's gut faded even as the superior smirk on Bradford's face increased. By the time they returned to the front door, the younger man was swaggering. But before he could get in Tucker's face, Esmerelda ordered him off with a spate of rapid-fire words.

Bradford glowered and retreated into the house while his mother held the door for Tucker. When he had stepped out onto the porch, which seemed far chillier than it had fifteen minutes earlier, she lifted a finger, and her dark brown eyes hardened to mahogany as she switched back to unaccented English. "Leave my boy alone, you hear? He's done nothing wrong. He might not have liked that other girl's father, but that doesn't make him a kidnapper. You go back to your station house and tell them he's innocent."

With that, she shut the door. Tucker heard the click of a dead bolt and the rattle of a chain, but his mind wasn't on such mundane things. It was focused on her last comment.

He might not have liked the other girl's father. Hell, that was news to Tucker. Had she meant Reginald Walsh, or one of the others? He turned back and raised his hand to knock, still convinced by the twist in his gut and the tension at the back of his neck that there was something here. Something he was missing.

But before his knock connected, his cell phone rang. He flipped it open. "McDermott."

"Why aren't you on your radio?" asked an unfamiliar female voice over a crackle of static.

He frowned, and tension coalesced in his gut. "Who is this? What's happened?"

"It's Maya Cooper. I'm at the hospital with Lizzie—

well, right now, I'm standing outside the hospital. I think you should get back to the station ASAP."

He was on his way to his SUV before she was done speaking. "What's wrong? Where's Alissa?" He didn't care that the question bordered on unprofessional.

A burst of static nearly drowned out Maya's reply, but he heard it well enough to panic.

"She's at the station. She's not answering her phone and someone just tripped the fire alarms!"

ONE MOMENT ALISSA WAS scanning the skull in relative peace and quiet. In the next, fire alarms whooped out of nowhere and the power cut out, plunging the windowless basement room into pitch-blackness broken only by a handful of LED lights shining for equipment that ran off backup batteries.

Her heart jammed into her throat, and she froze for a heartbeat, then grabbed for her weapon before realizing that she'd left it on her desk. She reeled in that direction and banged her shins on something sharp and solid.

"Where the hell are the emergency lights?" she said aloud, more to beat back the sudden creeps than because she expected an answer.

But a reply came at her out of the darkness, a sibilant hiss of breath and rough, masculine tones that filtered beneath the sound of the fire alarm. "I took care of them. A nice touch, don't you think?"

Alissa screamed and spun, flailing with her hands in the hope of finding the desk or the man. Her eyes finally adjusted and she saw a moving silhouette, a tall, wide-shouldered mass coming at her with deadly intent. She shouted and reeled back until she slammed into the desk.

But still the dark figure bore down on her.

Heart pounding, hands shaking as much from anger as fear, she grabbed for her gun, instead knocking a pile off her desk. Pencils and pens, papers and books fell to the floor with a clatter that was drowned out beneath the continued whoop of alarms.

Then it was too late for the gun, too late for her. The dark figure closed and grabbed for her. Part trained fighter, part terrified woman, Alissa yanked her knee up. The jab caught her attacker left of center, hard enough to drive him back a pace, but not enough to drop him.

"Bitch!" He lunged forward, grabbed her around the waist and slammed her to the floor.

Alissa's vision dimmed, then shot colors in her ringing head. Her lungs locked for want of air, and yesterday's bruises howled. *Get up!* her brain screamed, *Get up and fight!* But her dazed limbs wouldn't respond as she waited for the knockout blow.

It didn't come. He turned away and she heard him move across the room. A moment later the battery-powered emergency light near the doorway snapped on, giving the room a strange, eerie cast. The alarms shut off—maybe a coincidence, maybe not—and she heard fire engines approaching fast.

"We've got to move quickly. They'll be here any minute," he said, and returned to bend over Alissa. Her vision was badly blurred, giving her little to work with except shapes and sounds. His voice didn't seem familiar, but then, would it? She was an artist. She remembered faces, not sounds.

"Ferguson? Is that you?" She struggled to lift her spinning head from the floor. "Ferguson, you piece of garbage, I'll—"

Duct tape ripped nearby, and a rough hand and a sticky piece of tape silenced her midsentence. She screamed through her nose and one untaped corner of her mouth, and thrashed when he grabbed her and flipped her onto her stomach.

Adrenaline cleared the dizziness, but it was too late. Her hands were already bound, along with her ankles. Boots thundered overhead, firemen most likely, bringing a spurt of hope. She lifted her legs and smashed them into one of the blastproof gun lockers. The insulated metal cabinet reverberated with a satisfying crash, but the man only chuckled.

"Don't worry, it won't be long now. In fact, let me leave you with the anticipation." He crouched down beside her and positioned a flat, oblong box near her head. He flicked a switch, and a digital display snapped to life, black numbers against a brown-gray background.

It read 1:14. As she watched, it silently ticked down to 1:13. Then 1:12.

The man chuckled again. "Sorry, Officer Wyatt. It's nothing personal, but you've become part of the plan." Then he left, his footsteps echoing unhurriedly in the hallway.

Leaving her alone with the bomb.

TUCKER ABANDONED the SUV in the overfull street outside the police department. He tossed the keys to the first junior officer he saw. "Park it somewhere safe."

Then he plunged into the sea of bodies, straining to glimpse unruly honey-blond waves tamed beneath a ball cap. But most of the gathered, chattering throng was made up of support staff. He caught snatches of excited conversation as he passed.

"…fire in the upstairs conference room. Can you imagine…"

"They should have it under control in a min…"

"…could something like this happen? I can't believe…"

Driven by the gossip and by the knot in his gut that told him *this* was the action his instincts had foreseen, Tucker pushed toward the front door. Fat canvas hoses snaked up the granite steps, and a pall of greasy black smoke hung on the air.

Tucker saw Pendelton, the desk clerk who'd passed along the kidnapper's first note—was it only the morning before? He grabbed the junior officer by the shirtfront. "Where's Alissa?" When the kid's eyes went from surprised to baffled, Tucker cranked the volume and shouted. "Wyatt? Where's Officer Wyatt?"

"She's…she's," the clerk stuttered, baffled. "I dunno. Out in the field?"

Rage slammed through Tucker in an instant. If the BCCPD hadn't been so intent on disliking the three women of the Forensics Department, they would have known where the hell she was. He grabbed Pendelton by the collar. "She was in the basement working!"

Then, realizing that was no help, Tucker shoved the young man aside and bolted toward the building. He heard a volley of shouts and dodged the first firefighter who blocked his path. When the next firefighter grabbed Tucker's arm, he shook the guy off and shouted, "There's a woman down in the basement. I think she's in trouble!"

He was sure of it. The bastard must have set a fire in the station house to smoke her out, or else to smoke everyone else out and leave her behind. Alone.

On that last grim thought, Tucker lunged down the stairs, barely touching the treads in his need to reach her. "Alissa! Alissa, are you down here?"

He heard a loud clanging noise and ran harder.

The air was clear, with none of the greasy smoke that fouled the ground level. But the hall was nearly pitch-black, with no sign of the emergency lights, save one.

Heart hammering, Tucker charged into the office Alissa shared with her friends. The single light illuminated the scene. Alissa lay on the floor with her wrists taped behind her back, her ankles bound and her mouth covered with another strip of adhesive. Her eyes were wide and scared, and sweat beaded her brow. She tried to shout a muffled command through her nose, but there was no need. He'd seen it.

The device rested beside her head, ticking down from 0:07 to 0:06.

There was no time to think, barely any time to act. 0:05.

The station house was old and solid, the basement a box of reinforced concrete. Even if they made it to the stairs, the blast force would follow them, squeezed inside the cement structure.

0:04…0:03.

Knowing it was their only chance, Tucker grabbed Alissa off the floor, shoved her in the nearby gun locker, wedged himself into the narrow space and slammed the door.

He wrapped his arms around her and hung on tight.

And the world exploded around them.

Chapter Eight

The explosion sounded like a thousand high-speed trains colliding. The slap of concussion battered at Alissa, driving the air from her lungs and the strength from her body.

She burrowed into Tucker as the heat in the gun locker increased too far, too fast, until she was sure her clothes would crisp off her body. Her airways locked down and she couldn't breathe. She was almost too dazed to struggle against the encroaching blackness, the unconsciousness that seemed kinder than staying awake. But the strong arms around her waist and the feel of the man against her kept her upright, kept her fighting.

The initial thunder subsided, but the heat continued to build, as did the roaring around them. Her heart wailed for their brand-new equipment even as she struggled to free her bound hands and labored to suck in oxygen through her nearly blocked nose.

"Hold still, I've got it." Tucker shifted against her,

wedged one hand between their bodies and worked it up to her face. "Sorry about this."

He yanked the tape off quickly, but that wasn't saying much given the confines of the locker. She felt the burn of pulled hairs and torn skin, tasted a trickle of blood, but that was nothing compared to the blessed relief of air. She sucked in a lungful of hot, foul oxygen, and nearly wept.

"Sorry," he said again, as though any of this was his fault.

She shook her head, though it was pitch-black in the locker. "Don't apologize. You saved me."

And had nearly gotten himself fried in the process. She shuddered at the thought of what might have happened if he'd been a moment later.

Mistaking her shiver, he shifted away and worked his hands down to her wrists, which remained taped behind her back. "Here, let me."

With the move, she became suddenly, intimately aware that they were pressed together belly to belly, chest to chest. Her bound hands forced her breasts up and into him, and though she'd never considered her nipples a particularly important erogenous zone, her pebble-hard peaks rubbed against the solid plane of his chest and became hot, wanting buttons of pleasure.

The air outside the gun locker might have cooled a few degrees, but inside, the cramped space grew warmer with a new, spiky sexual energy. Thundering footfalls and shouts seemed to come from afar, as did short blasts from a fire extinguisher.

Moments away from tearing the duct tape that bound her, Tucker stilled, pressed intimately against her, hands holding her trapped wrists. The commotion outside announced the arrival of fire crews, but the noise seemed dimmed by the pounding of her heart. Excitement flared through her body, sexual energy composed of equal parts relief at being alive and naughty pleasure at the realization that far from being turned off by the restraints, she was completely, utterly turned on.

The low groan that vibrated from his chest to hers, and the hard length of him pressed up against her suggested he felt the same—excited, inflamed, even more so because their rescuers were mere feet away, separated from them by the closed door of the blast-proof gun locker.

"Tucker," she said softly, then fell silent because she had no idea what she wanted to say, whether she wanted to push him away or pull him closer, though acutely aware that she could do neither with her wrists bound.

"I know," he replied in the same quiet voice, neither of them ready to announce their presence to the firefighters who were working to subdue the blast fires outside.

Then he leaned in close, and the outside world backed off a step. His lips hovered above hers for a moment, felt but not seen in the darkness. His warm breath feathered across her cheek. "Sorry," he said again.

And kissed her.

Alissa's world detonated, fragmenting into bits of

color and flame behind her closed eyelids. She couldn't move, couldn't participate with anything but her lips and tongue, leaving her able to do nothing but accept the sensations flaring through her body as he dove in and hung on tight.

The fire between them reminded her of that first night, when they hadn't known each other at all. But it was hotter now, because they did know each other, and damned if she didn't like him. The knowledge consumed her, confused her, even as his hands slid down to grip her hips and hold her close to his hardness.

A wash of desire suffused her, and she parted her lips on a sigh, or maybe a plea. His tongue swept in on the motion, demanding a response she was already giving. She strained against her bonds and rubbed her aching breasts against him, glorying in his harsh groan and the clutch of his hands on her hips. The tape frustrated her and excited her at the same moment. The bonds opened her to the sensations but prevented her from completing their embrace, from twining her arms around his neck and hanging on for the ride.

She nearly moaned with the dark pleasure of it, and he broke away to slide his lips across her throat and nip at her earlobe. "They're coming."

It took a moment for her to process the words, for her to realize that the outside sounds were growing louder, the voices more distinct, the crackle of flames less obvious.

"We should stop," she said, though her tongue felt heavy on the words, her body aflame where it pressed against his. She hadn't forgotten why this was a bad idea, but the reasons all seemed less important than the reality of his body against hers, the taste of him on her tongue.

"For now," he agreed, but he dragged his hands up and down her body in one last inciting caress. "But later…?"

"Later," she agreed, thinking *to hell with it*. Why dance around any longer? She wanted him, he wanted her. They'd tried to avoid the fact since that first night at the dance club, and ignoring the chemistry had only served to intensify it, until the spark between them had become a conflagration that would not be denied.

"Later," he said. "Count on it."

With that, he ripped the tape binding her arms and swung open the door to the gun cabinet.

A nearby firefighter yelped and nearly dropped his canister of chemical suppressant, but Alissa didn't see any of the other reactions. She barely had time to register the total destruction of the workspace she and the other women had spent a month putting together just the way they liked it. Then the fumes, dust and smoke slapped her like a physical blow. She closed her eyes and raised her hands to her nose and mouth as she choked horribly.

She took a step forward, realized too late that her ankles were still taped, and pitched headlong out of the gun cabinet. Strong arms caught her as she fell and swung her up against a warm, hard chest.

Tucker carried her out of the office, coughing against the fumes and smoke. When firefighters moved to take her, he waved them away and kept going, not out the front door, where she knew a mob must be assembled, but out the back, to the relative quiet of the parking lot.

There he let her down to lean back against a stranger's car while he bent and untaped her ankles. When she was free, he rose and he stared down as though memorizing her, as though he could see down to her bones and flesh and assure himself that she was unharmed.

The raw worry in his expression touched something deep inside her, and she reached out and took his soot-streaked hand in a spontaneous gesture that felt as if it meant more than it should. "I'm okay."

"Good," he said flatly, his expression changing to rage, "because I'm not."

He pulled away from her and stalked to the building and then back. His hands were fisted at his sides and his shoulders vibrated with such an awful tension that she thought they might rip his flesh from his bones. He paced back and forth, back and forth, and then spun to drop down beside her on the hood of the car. The vehicle nearly buckled beneath his angry weight.

Alissa couldn't gauge his mood. She hadn't been around many angry men, and wasn't sure how to handle him.

Her parents had always fought behind closed doors, leaving her six-year-old self to hide beneath the covers or, once, press an ear to the door. Most of her relationships hadn't progressed past the blush of newness to that point where anger could be acknowledged or expressed. And she and Aiden had somehow avoided major conflicts.

Maybe, she thought now with a glimmer of surprise, that had been part of their problem. They hadn't cared enough to invoke strong emotions like anger.

Or passion.

She felt a primal, atavistic thrill when Tucker cursed and thumped the hood with his fists. But when he turned to her, and all that restless, edgy temper was in his eyes, the thrill sparked to something different. Something deeper and more dangerous.

She nearly launched herself at him, irrespective of who they were, where they were. But because of who and where, she turned away and stared at the back entrance to the station, which looked nearly normal, giving no hint of the danger within. "He destroyed the skull." And had nearly destroyed her in the process. But which of those things had been the ultimate goal?

Regardless, her comment did what she'd intended. It focused them on the case, not each other.

Tucker was silent for so long that she looked back at him, and saw the reluctant agreement in his eyes. He inclined his head. "We'll talk about it later, then."

It was more a vow than a date, and the promise of it left her close to trembling. But instead of giving in to the urge, she stood and jerked her head toward the street. "Come on. Let's find Chief Parry and the task force. This is going to change a few things."

It CHANGED a hell of a lot of things, Tucker realized once the task force was assembled in the conference room. It didn't change the basics—they were still stumbling around in the dark on this case, with too many questions and too few concrete answers. But the second incident at the BCCPD station cemented one irrefutable fact.

This was personal. It wasn't just about the girls. It was about the cops, too.

It was about Alissa.

He kept watch on her from two rows back. They all wore their coats because the conference room windows were open to air out the smoke and fumes from the bathroom bomb that had been used to trip the fire alarms. Alissa looked lost within her puffy parka, but when Chief Parry gestured, she squared her shoulders and rose to stand at the front of the room.

She glanced at Tucker, a quick look that told him she was feeling shakier than she'd let on. Cassie and Maya were both in the field, leaving her alone.

No, Tucker thought, not alone. She had him.

Don't be an idiot, his conscience snapped, *she doesn't have you. Nobody has you, and it's better off that way. You don't stick. You never stick.*

"Yeah, and I like it that way," Tucker muttered, earning himself a few curious glances.

At the front of the room, Alissa linked her hands together in front of her body and said, "I should probably apologize for attracting Johnny Ferguson to Bear Claw, if that's who our perp winds up being. But I'm not going to." There were a few frowns as she continued. "Not because I feel good about what's happened. Maria Blackhorse and Holly Barrett are still missing, and Lizzie's recovery is going to be a long one. There's nothing good about that, or about the bombs that destroyed my vehicle and the equipment downstairs." She paused and swallowed. "However, while the past couple of months have by no means been easy for me, I have learned to respect the BCCPD." Her lips quirked. "You can be unfriendly as hell, but you're good cops."

A grumble rose in the room, but Tucker thought it was tinged with a hint of regret. Part of him wondered whether this case had dragged on so long precisely because of their behavior toward the new additions.

"And because you're good cops," Alissa continued, "I have every faith that we're going to catch this bastard." The silence that greeted her announcement was perhaps warmer than the mutters, but couldn't be considered friendly by any stretch. After a moment she sighed. "Okay, so that didn't work."

"It was a good try, though," Tucker said aloud before he could stop himself. He earned a couple of chuckles and sidelong glances, but the room warmed a few degrees, and he thought he saw Captain Parry nod.

Alissa shrugged as though she wasn't quite sure whether he was helping or not, and said, "Okay then, on to the bad news. The skull is gone, and the computer images I had taken of it were wiped by the blast and the fire. Most of the new equipment is toast, and I can't tell you a damn thing about the guy who attacked me, except that he was about six feet, two hundred pounds and had a mean right cross."

Tucker wasn't the only one who winced at the image, but he was probably the only one who vowed in that moment to kill the bastard when they caught him.

Chief Parry frowned. "Could it have been Ferguson?"

Alissa tucked her hands into her pockets and seemed to shrink slightly, until her face was a pale dot against her dark blue parka. "It could have been. But I wouldn't testify to it." Which meant more to her than most, Tucker knew.

"Isn't she supposed to be a facial expert?" Piedmont grumbled behind Tucker. "How can she not know if it was the guy?"

The careless question scraped along Tucker's nerve endings and jabbed right into his sense of fair play, which he admitted had so far been lacking when it came to the members of the new Forensics Department. He spun and snapped, "Because it was dark and she was nearly unconscious. Then, by the time she was fully conscious, her hands, feet and mouth were bound with duct tape, and the bastard had put a bomb a foot away from her head. You do the math."

The room went dead quiet and Tucker realized he'd spoken louder than he'd intended. But when Piedmont's face reddened with anger, he realized it was about time. This crap had gone on long enough, and it was hurting the PD's effectiveness. Captain Parry had tried the subtle way. Now it was Tucker's turn.

And he was anything but subtle.

He stood and scowled down at Piedmont, then the

others, seeing that their faces reflected anything from amusement to anger. He focused on the angry faces and felt his own temper flare to match. "Enough is enough, people. We may not have liked how or why Fitz left, but he's gone. Last I heard, he was deep-sea fishing off St. Petersburg. He's moved on—why can't we?" He gestured back at Alissa without looking at her. "Even if the kidnapper turns out to be Johnny Ferguson, it's not Wyatt's fault that he snatched those girls. She did her level best to put him behind bars. And it's not her fault he came in here and trashed the place. Hell, it's our fault for not protecting her better when we knew she was a target."

That one hit a little close to home as Tucker's conscience told him he should have stayed, should have protected her. But he'd needed the space and the distance to combat the pull between them.

Half a dozen of the assembled cops looked away from Tucker's glare or shifted uncomfortably in their chairs. But the others stared at him with varying degrees of hostility. Piedmont climbed to his feet and got in Tucker's face. "That's an awful long list of things that aren't her fault, McDermott. And why the hell are you defending her all of a sudden?" His face darkened and turned sly. "Or does it have something to do with that little scene down by the lake last night? You two were down there long enough for the snow to wipe your footprints."

Rage reddened Tucker's vision. He wanted to grab the guy and put him up against a wall—hard—but restrained himself. That would only add fuel to rumors that didn't need additional kindling. Instead he forced his voice to be level. "I'm not going to dignify that. But I am going to say that if anyone else wants to take a jab at Wyatt, they're going to have to go through me first."

"And what about once you're gone?" Piedmont asked. "Everyone knows you're a lame duck, just like the boys up in Rock Creek know you'll be moving on from there in three years or so. Isn't that your usual time frame?"

"Enough!" Chief Parry's voice cracked whip-snap, silencing the room.

Into that quiet, Alissa said, "The Forensics Department takes care of itself and its own. I don't need Detective McDermott's interference." She advanced on Piedmont without sparing Tucker a glance. "If you have a problem with me or my police work, be a man and bring it to me. If not, then grow up and get over the fact that technology has moved on without you. Cassie, Maya and I are trying to drag your butts out of the investigative Dark Ages. Got it?"

Piedmont's face reddened and his hands fisted at his sides. The air crackled with tension, and Tucker moved to Alissa's side, ready to level the guy if he so much as lifted a finger.

Captain Parry barked, "Sit down, all of you!"

He stood and took the front of the room, waving the others back to their seats. This time Tucker sat beside Alissa, in the space usually occupied by her girlfriends.

"Clearly, I should have done this a long time ago,"

Parry snapped, "but I kept hoping you guys would work this out among yourselves. Apparently, that was giving you too much credit." He divided his glare equally among the assembled cops. "So I'll say it one last time, and I expect this to be the end of things. Fitzroy O'Malley retired voluntarily. Nobody asked him to leave, nobody pressured him to make room for the new department. I would have been pleased to have him stay on as long as he wanted, to act in an advisory capacity. He declined. Period. End of story."

Alissa shifted at Tucker's side, but when he glanced at her delicate profile, he couldn't read anything beyond agitation.

Parry continued before any of the others could comment. "The Forensics Department is here to stay, people, so get used to it. You don't have to love Wyatt, Cooper or Dumont, but you'd bloody well better figure out how to work with them." He flicked his glare to Alissa. "And that goes for you and your team, too." He transferred his attention to the room at large. "The BCCPD is a unit. Figure out how to make it work, or else."

The total silence that followed Parry's threat was tribute to a leader who most often guided by example and calm suggestion, and had been pushed to his limits.

Tucker saw a few shamed faces, a few sullen ones. The mood was uncertain and tense, like the woman beside him.

"Now," Parry said briskly, clapping his hands together. "Moving on. McDermott's follow-up visit with Bradford Croft didn't gain much either way, so he'll stay on our 'maybe' list. There've been no sightings of Ferguson, who remains at the top of the list. We've got a run-down of local prefab shed dealers and got a hit on Michael Swopes. He only bought one, but it's something, so he moves to the head of the class, too." Parry paused and lowered his voice a notch. "I know we're all tense. Hell, we have a kidnapper in our town, and two girls are still missing. I get all that. But tearing at each other isn't the answer. Working together is." With that, he jerked his head at the door. "Go on. Get to work."

But when Tucker and Alissa rose to follow the others, the chief held up a hand. "You two stay."

While the others departed, Tucker lowered his voice and stepped close to their boss. "Sir? I'd like to explain about last night. You see—"

"I don't care about that," Parry interrupted. "Rumors happen, especially in mixed-sex partnerships. Deal with the gossip—and any problems—on your own time." He didn't gesture them to chairs or into his office, so the three of them stood in the conference room, huddled inside their jackets as the sharp winter air whistled through the open windows and battled the sharp taint of smoke and destruction. "No, I want to talk about protection for both of you."

Tucker moved a half step closer to Alissa. "No protection necessary. We'll watch each other's backs."

It wasn't that he didn't trust the capability of the other cops, but quite frankly, he didn't trust their mental states at this point. The force was too fragmented by internal pettiness. It still burned in his gut that nobody had bothered to check for Alissa when the PD was evacuated. If he hadn't gone looking for her...

He shuddered at the thought of the blast, then again at the memory of what had transpired between them afterward. Maybe it the touch of her parka against his leather jacket, or the fresh, feminine scent that brushed his nostrils and relieved the taint of the bombs. Whatever the reason, he was acutely, elementally aware of her beside him. The depth of that awareness paralyzed him for an instant, one in which he realized that somehow, impossibly, she had become important to him. And what the hell was he going to do about that?

Nothing, he told himself fiercely while the conversation moved on without him. *You're going to keep your hands off her, because she doesn't need another disappointment in her life.*

A pair of images rose unbidden in his mind—his mother and Helen. Both wore identical looks of sadness, souring his gut and pinching his conscience.

"I want to go after Ferguson, Chief," Alissa said, jolting Tucker out of his painful moment of self-awareness.

"I know you do," Parry replied, "but the needs of the task force would be better served using you elsewhere. You're a crime-scene specialist, remember? Approach it from that direction and stop trying to be a beat cop." He glanced at Tucker, and his eyes held a faint challenge, or maybe a warning. "Help her with whatever she needs. Beg, borrow or steal the necessary equipment. And whatever you do, don't leave her alone again. Ferguson—or whoever he is—has a bad habit of waltzing into and out of the PD like he belongs here."

The guarded look in Parry's eyes and Alissa's hiss of indrawn breath told Tucker the others had come to the same conclusion he had. It was possible they weren't looking for Ferguson at all.

It was possible their kidnapper was a cop.

Chapter Nine

Stung by the chief's implication that she'd forgotten to focus on her specialty, and stunned by the thought of an inside job—Alissa stumbled down the stairs to the basement, eyes stinging with the smoke and chemical funk. The stinging became tears when she ducked under the caution tape and stepped inside what was left of the Forensics Department offices.

Much of Cassie's equipment had survived, thanks to being in the next room over, but the shock wave was likely to have messed with the delicate computer chips and fine-tuned instruments. There was no way the machines could be trusted to give accurate readings until they'd been examined and recalibrated by an expert.

The computers and Alissa's equipment had sustained the brunt of the blast. She winced at the sight of strewn, blackened papers and the remains of her scanner, which had been blast-gutted and burned to an unrecognizable tangle of metal and melted plastic. There was no trace of the skull, which had been one of their few solid leads.

The failure ate at her. The evidence had been lost on her watch, leaving them with more questions than answers. The bomb squad would work the room as soon as they finished with the other sites, but the analysis would take time.

Time that Maria Blackhorse and Holly Barrett didn't have.

Alissa cursed under her breath and dashed the tears away. Though the chief's comments had hurt, he might just have a point. She was a crime-scene specialist, damn it, and so far she'd been doing very little with the scenes. So she should get to it. She should find herself a quiet spot and go over what was left of her notes and photographs, her impressions and images.

Even as she thought about it, she felt a tingle in her chest, a "click" of connection she hadn't yet felt on this case. Her gut suddenly told her that she'd seen something. Perceived something that her brain might not even have fully registered, might not have understood at the time. But what?

Footsteps sounded in the hallway, too quick and light to be Tucker, who had remained upstairs with Chief Parry. Alissa spun, adrenaline kicking through her, washing away the aches and pains with an instant-fight reflex.

Cassie stood in the doorway, eyes stark in her pale face. She rushed into the room, hands outstretched. "'Lissa! I just heard. Are you okay?"

Alissa leaned into her friend's embrace, but where tears had threatened moments earlier, now she felt hollow and drained, as though she was running out of fight. Another set of footsteps—heels, this time— rushed down the stairs and Maya burst into the room. She joined the hug without a word, and Alissa let herself relax for half a second, knowing that these friends, at least, wouldn't let her down.

Neither will Tucker, a small voice whispered at the back of her head, but she quickly squelched the thought. Tucker was guaranteed to let her down. The only difference from her past experiences was that it wouldn't be a surprise when it happened.

As though conjured by his name in her mind, Tucker stepped from the shadowed hallway. She didn't know how long he'd been there, or how he'd approached with none of the warning the others had given her. His eyes were dark and intent, his too-long hair and gliding walk only serving to reinforce the image he projected, of wildness in captivity, of a predator in man's clothing.

His appearance reminded her of the look on his face as he'd grabbed her and shoved her in the gun locker, the heat of their bodies when he'd crowded in beside her, and the way he'd stood up for her in the meeting, in a thoroughly uncharacteristic and unexpected manner.

Almost as though he cared.

Heart racing, Alissa pulled away from Cassie and Maya. She wanted to go to him with as much urgency as she wanted to run away. So instead, she stood motionless as another man joined him in the doorway. A stranger.

Cassie stiffened and cursed under her breath, earning a surprised look from Maya.

"Sorry," Cass muttered, though she didn't look sorry at all. "But my new *assistant*," she sneered the word, "is more annoying in person than he was on the phone."

There was a layer of something deeper beneath Cassie's customary I-don't-want-anyone-helping-me attitude, causing Alissa to give the stranger—presumably the FBI evidence specialist, Seth Varitek—a second look.

She had to admit that the men crowding just inside the ruined office made a striking pair. Tucker looked like leashed violence. In contrast, Seth Varitek projected rock solidness, as though not even a tornado would move him. He was an inch shorter than Tucker, but probably outweighed him by another twenty pounds of muscle. Varitek's down-filled parka added even more mass, and his heavily muscled, jeans-clad legs were slightly spread, anchoring him to the floor.

Where Tucker vibrated with intensity, keeping his weight on the balls of his feet as though ready to spin and parry a blow at a moment's notice, Varitek stood rooted, as though he would take the punch and return it tenfold.

The evidence specialist's features were surprisingly pleasant, rough-hewn but saved from forbidding by his eyes, which were the palest green, surrounded by a darker ring and intensified by long, black lashes.

Of the two men, Alissa preferred Tucker's leashed wildness, the streak of unpredictability that excited her, challenged her. And that was part of the problem, wasn't it? She didn't go for the solid sort. She went for the skittish men, the ones that bolted without warning.

Or in this case, with warning but little remorse.

Cassie stepped away from Maya and made a face before she jerked her chin toward the door. "I don't suppose one of you wants to show him around?"

"What's to show him?" Alissa said with a quick slash of bitterness. "We're done here. Finished. Our grant money is gone, along with all our equipment." Her throat closed on the words, but she wouldn't shame herself with tears. Not in front of Tucker or the stranger. But her voice was husky when she said, "I'm so damn sorry, guys."

It hit her then in a way she'd managed to hold off for so long. This was at least partly her fault. She'd attracted the kidnapper's attention, and in trying to get at her, he'd destroyed the space they'd worked so hard to fund, then build.

"No," Cassie said quickly, attitude dissolving as she touched Alissa's forearm. "This isn't about you. It's about some sick jerk who's breaking the law. You can't take responsibility for him. You can't."

"You're right. Intellectually I know you're right." Alissa sucked back a sigh and shook her head. "But it's so hard not to think—"

"Then don't," Tucker interrupted from the doorway. "Don't think about it. Insurance will replace the equipment eventually, and you'll find a way to manage until then. Don't overstress it, just do your job and move on."

Stung, confused, heartsick, Alissa lifted her chin. "That's easy for you to say, isn't it?" Then she shook her head. "I'm sorry. That was uncalled for."

He looked away. "We should go. Parry gave us our assignments."

Yes, and hers had been to do her job. Crime-scene analysis. But with half of her notes destroyed, and much of the evidence gone in the blast, what was left to analyze? A few photographs and memories, most likely. But if that was what she had left, that was what she would work with. So she waved to the doorway. "You guys go ahead. I want to talk to Maya for a minute." She included Cassie in the statement, though planned to apologize—and find out what was up with this Varitek guy—later.

Tucker didn't budge. "You can talk upstairs."

"No. It has to be down here." Alissa met his eyes. "Please."

It was less a request and more an acknowledgment of his concern, but Tucker's eyes darkened. He nodded. "I'll be upstairs running the security tapes of the lobby and the parking lot from the past three days. The bastard's got to be on there somewhere." But his voice held less hope than his words, telling her that he felt it, too—a sense that their quarry remained a frustrating few steps ahead of them.

"I could stay," Cassie said weakly, reluctance evident in every line of her body. "We should check and see what's salvageable."

"None of it," Varitek said, his deep voice sounding

solid, like the rest of him. "And you should let the insurance adjusters have at it first. The case is priority-one."

Cassie flushed and spun to him, hands fisted. "Don't tell me how to do my job. Just because you've got some extra letters after your name doesn't make you—"

"The man offering to scare up a mobile evidence unit for you?" he interrupted smoothly.

"You— Oh." Cass swallowed. "Thanks. That would be… Thanks."

Unused to seeing her friend flustered by anyone, especially not by a man, Alissa watched with great interest as Varitek jerked his head toward the stairs leading up out of the basement. "Come on. I'll make some calls after you show me around."

It was a challenge and a subtle bribe rolled into one. And to Alissa's surprise, Cassie inclined her head. "Deal." But as she passed Varitek in the doorway, she paused and looked up at him. "Don't think this means I like you, though."

The big man paused a moment as though thinking, then shrugged. "Don't think I care either way."

Cassie's curse followed them both from the room, sending a kink of worry through Alissa's chest. "She is *not* going to be happy about that arrangement."

"Don't worry," Tucker said from his edgy position near the door, not quite inside, but not quite gone, either, "I crossed paths with Varitek once before. He's a good man. Loyal. Steady. He'll take care of your friend."

"That's what I'm afraid of," Alissa said wryly.

"Cassie doesn't take kindly to being sheltered. She had enough of that growing up." She was aware of Maya standing quietly nearby, of Tucker's larger-than-life presence in the doorway. "Speaking of which, that's your cue to leave. Maya and I have work to do."

"The room hasn't been processed for evidence yet." Tucker shifted away from the door frame, but didn't step further into the room.

"You think I don't know that?" Alissa's voice was sharper than she'd intended, but the nerves were building now at the thought of what she was about to do. "Give me some credit. We won't touch anything." When he didn't move, she blew out a frustrated breath. "Just go, okay? I'll be fine, and you have surveillance footage to review."

"Right," he agreed, but didn't move. He stared at her until her entire world seemed made up of dark eyes and near breakpoint tension. Then he nodded and turned away. "I'll be upstairs."

His feet echoed hollowly on the stairs. When he was gone, Alissa turned to Maya, who knew as much as anyone about the workings of the human mind, and said, "Okay, I need you to hypnotize me and take me back to the attack. I'm pretty sure there's something in my head, some clue I'm missing."

Maya's lovely face darkened. "Are you sure? Remember what happened the last time we tried this?"

Alissa nearly shuddered at the memory of the time Maya had hypnotized her to get at the root of a series of nightmares and had gotten the whole sordid story of her father's disappearance, instead. "I remember." Then she squared her shoulders. "And I'm sure. I'm not letting anyone else get hurt if I can help it."

"All right." Maya gestured to the floor. "Let's sit cross-legged. Get yourself as comfortable as possible."

Alissa did as she was told and tried to stem the feeling of rising panic. But what was the alternative? With much of the evidence destroyed, and a conviction building in her gut that she'd seen something she wasn't remembering, there was no other way. So she settled and closed her eyes.

God, she hated hypnosis.

UPSTAIRS, TUCKER FORCED HIMSELF to concentrate on the surveillance tapes while he kept half an ear on the radio chatter at the front desk.

Mendoza and Piedmont thought they had a lead on Johnny Ferguson. The Tecumseh PD had tracked down an ex-girlfriend who had claimed no clue of his whereabouts until she realized he'd swiped her credit cards and her stash of ready cash. The cards had been used five times, at gas stations, all on the major roads leading from Tecumseh to Bear Claw.

Just that morning, one of the cards had been used to rent a room at the Shady Lady Motel on the other side of Bear Claw Mountain.

Suddenly things were starting to come together.

Tucker itched to be in on the collar. He wanted an opportunity to plant his fist in the bastard's face, for Alissa's sake. For the sake of the kidnapped girls.

Instead he forced himself to sit still and fast-forward through hours of tape, knowing Alissa was downstairs, and knowing that he might not be lucky enough to save her a second time if the perp got inside their guard. Some of the evidence pointed to Ferguson as their kidnapper. He had revenge as his motive, and the credit card purchase indicated that he was in the area, giving him opportunity. But not all the pieces fit, not all the questions were answered.

How had he gotten into the PD so easily, not once, but three separate times? And if the ultimate target was Alissa, then why kidnap the girls at all? Why send the first note to Tucker instead of directly to her? And did the kidnapper have the necessary bomb-making skills? Sawyer, the grizzled leader of the bomb squad, still maintained that the devices were the work of a pro.

Tucker frowned as hours of irrelevant faces and actions scrolled past on the video monitor. Nothing. He strained to hear a report from the motel. Also nothing.

He wanted to drive out and see for himself. He wanted to rise and pace, wanted to return to the basement and—

Hell, he didn't know what he wanted to do anymore, only that his desires and his professional instincts were getting tangled up in each other. He was protecting his partner, yes, but he also wanted to be near her.

He was halfway out of his seat when the phone at his elbow rang. He picked up the handset automatically, tensed for news though he'd heard nothing on the radio. "McDermott."

"Tucker! Good to speak with you. It's Chief White-thorne."

Hell. His new boss. Tucker forced himself to sit, and collect his thoughts. "Yes, sir. It's good to hear from you."

In reality, the call was damned inconvenient and he wished he hadn't answered. He'd been putting off Whitethorne for nearly a month now, unwilling to leave Bear Claw until the kidnapper had been brought to justice.

"I'm calling to check on your ETA. We're plenty busy up here, and we could use another good cop. That's why we hired you," Whitethorne said without preamble. His plain speech and solid police work were two of the main reasons Tucker had chosen Rock Creek for his transfer.

"I know. I'm sorry." At a spate of radio speak, Tucker shifted the phone to his other ear and tried to catch the update. No sign of Ferguson at the Shady Lady Motel. Aware of Whitethorne's expectant silence, and doubly aware that he'd held his new boss off too long already, Tucker said, "We're closing in on this guy. One of the kidnapped girls is home, but the other two are still out there. Worse, he's started taking potshots at members of the task force." At one in particular, but he was oddly reluctant to discuss Alissa with his new employer.

There was a moment of silence, then Whitethorne's voice, tinged with regret. "Listen, Tucker. I know you're involved with something big, but we hired you two months ago and we're running thin. I need you here, or else I need to know that you're not coming so I can find someone else."

And there it was, decision time at the moment Tucker felt least able to make a decision. The pressure of it itched along his skin in restless waves, making him want to pace, making him want to move and keep on moving.

Whitethorne was right. He needed to make a decision, he'd let this drag on too long. What was keeping him in Bear Claw? With Varitek involved, the task force didn't really need him. Someone else could watch out for Alissa.

It would be better for her if he left now. Better for him. If he stayed…

Hell, if he stayed, he'd act on the promise of her kiss in the gun locker and their whispered agreement afterward. *Later.* They would lose themselves in each other, and for a while it would be good. Then it would be not so good. She would want him to stay, and he would try to want the same thing. Who knew? It might even work for a while. But in time, the restlessness would come as it always did. He'd resent her for holding him in one place; she'd hate him for wanting to go. It would end badly. He'd been there before and didn't want to go back there again, for both their sakes.

So he pinched the bridge of his nose with his free hand and said, "I'll be there the day after tomorrow. You have my word on it."

But as he hung up the phone, Tucker didn't feel the slightest bit better about his decision.

Damned if part of him didn't want to stay.

"OKAY. YOU FEELING relaxed now?"

Maya's voice seemed to come to Alissa from a floaty place far away, though paradoxically, her brain felt razor sharp. "Yep," she answered. "Relaxed."

Maya claimed that her technique wasn't precisely hypnosis, more like deep relaxation and gentle questioning, but Alissa had never been quite sure of the distinction between the two. The end result was the same—near total recall.

"Okay. I want you to look over at your desk chair and tell me what you see. Not how it looks now, but how it looked earlier today, when you first came into the office after the morning meeting."

Part of Alissa seemed to sit aside from the process and blush as she described the office and her musings about Tucker. The hypnosis—or whatever it was—stripped away her natural reticence and laid her bare for scrutiny. She trusted Maya as much as she trusted anyone, but the process left her feeling naked. Vulnerable.

"Now, tell me about the man," Maya's voice asked. "What did he look like?"

Alissa recoiled from the memory of hard hands and a stinging blow. "I don't know. It was too dark. There weren't any windows, no light except for the machines." Equipment that was now trash, her active mind told her as it raced along seemingly faster than the sleepy beat of her heart. "I didn't see anything, didn't see—"

"Take it easy," Maya ordered, voice soothing.

"Breathe. You're doing great. What else do you remember?"

"Feet." The word popped out before Alissa was even aware of thinking it. "I remember his feet."

"What about his feet?"

"I'm…I'm not sure." Alissa frowned, concentrating, but the image wouldn't stay clear. Then, as though a slide projector had been triggered, the image slid to one of another place, another pair of feet.

"Daddy?" she said in an almost childish voice. "Why are you wearing your good shoes? Where are you going?" The detached part of her consciousness cringed at the question, and at the grief when she said, "He told me he was going away for a while, that he'd send for me when he could. But he lied. He had another family that he liked better than ours."

"Alissa." Maya's voice called through the layered images and the tears that crowded her throat, making it hard to breathe. "Alissa, I need you to concentrate on something else now, okay? I need you to come back into this room and think about what you saw in here today. You said you were missing something. That you'd seen something and you needed to remember."

"Right." That was the weird, schizophrenic thing about Maya's technique. On one level Alissa was completely aware of her surroundings, Maya's request and its importance. Yet on another level she was six years old again, watching her father pull on his Rockies jacket and ball cap and heft the single duffel he'd taken when he'd left.

He'd plucked her first-grade picture from beneath its magnet on the white refrigerator, she remembered. He'd glanced at her, tucked it into the bag and said, "So I won't be lonely until I see you again."

Except she hadn't seen him. He hadn't come for her. Hadn't called. He'd quite simply disappeared from her life.

Poof.

"Alissa?" Maya's voice was gently chiding. "Alissa, I need you to focus." Then she paused and her voice softened to curious. "Or maybe I don't. Tell me what you see now."

"Feet again," Alissa answered. One part of her was baffled by the sudden foot fetish while another stared at the heavy work boots. "I don't recognize them, though."

"Look up. Let yourself look up and see who the feet are attached to."

"Good idea." In her mind's eye, Alissa told herself to look up and higher still. She saw the image of a man superimposed over the true image of the bomb-damaged room around them. He was tall and whip-thin, with long arms and wide-palmed hands. When she got to his face, it fogged over for a moment, then cleared and she gasped.

"Who is it?" Maya asked quickly.

Alissa clenched her fists and reminded herself that it was nothing more than a memory and a memory couldn't hurt her. "It's Ferguson."

"Are you sure?"

"Positive," the analytical part of her answered, "but it's not right. He's not anchored in the scene. It's more like he's floating through it, work boots and all." It was the boots that kept drawing her attention, though she didn't know why.

"Then he's probably a suggestion," Maya said, voice reflecting disappointment. "Your brain put him there because it's logical, not necessarily because he was there."

"Probably." Alissa swallowed when she saw another figure behind Ferguson, this one broad-shouldered and dangerous, though on a different level. She heard her voice grow thin and worried when she asked, "Can I wake up now?"

Maya's tone sharpened with interest. "Why? What are you seeing?"

"It's Tucker." The too-aware portion of Alissa mentally screamed in embarrassment as the soft, vulnerable part of her confessed, "He's saving me. We're in the gun locker, and the bomb is going off. Now we're kissing. His hands are on my breasts and I don't want him to stop. He—"

"Okay! I get it." There was a thread of shocked laughter in Maya's voice. "I'm going to count up now, and when I get to five, I want you to wake all the way up. Okay? One...two..."

She snapped her fingers on "five," and Alissa regained herself. She immediately slammed her eyelids shut and groaned aloud as her face flamed what felt like a hundred shades of crimson. "I can't believe I said that! Please, please, please tell me you were the only one that heard it."

"I was the only one who heard you," Maya said dutifully. "Open your eyes, I promise I won't tease. I won't even mention it. We can concentrate on the other stuff you remembered."

"Like feet, my father leaving and a man who might or might not be Johnny Ferguson." Alissa opened her eyes and swore softly. "Not much help."

"Maybe we're not looking at it correctly." Maya pursed her lips.

"Sorry," Alissa said. "It's not you, it's me. I'm…not very good at hypnosis, or whatever this is." This was the second time they'd tried the technique for cases. The first had proven helpful, but the important information had been buried amidst garbage about her father.

"Not true." Maya unfolded herself and rose gracefully to her feet, then leaned down to offer Alissa a hand. "You're very susceptible, which is both good and bad. Good because you usually come away with more than you brought in. Bad because sometimes you don't come away with precisely what you wanted."

"Understatement of the week," Alissa grumbled, allowing Maya to help her to her feet. "My father is such old news it's ridiculous, and Tucker…" Though she hadn't meant to talk about him, once the name was out there, hanging on the smoke-hazed air, she shrugged. "We had that…encounter a few months ago at the club, remember?"

Maya lifted an elegant eyebrow, and a faint smile

touched her lips. "Of course I remember, 'Lissa. It all but vibrates in the room when you two are within twenty feet of each other."

"Oh. Well." Alissa swallowed, not liking the sound of that. She started to say that it made no sense, that it wasn't a good idea for her to get involved with Tucker. Instead she jammed her hands in the pockets of her winter coat and felt suddenly warm when she said, "I haven't been with anyone since Aiden."

Cassie might have screeched, *Too much information,* because for all their closeness, the three women rarely shared intimate secrets. But Maya, being Maya, simply nodded. "And now you're thinking in those terms with Tucker. Is that wise?"

Alissa snorted. "Hell, no. And stop using your counselor's voice with me. I'm not going to freak out. I'm just—" she blew out a breath "—I don't know what I am. Confused, I suppose. What I want to do and what I should do are two different things right now. That doesn't happen to me very often."

"So what are you going to do?"

Alissa shrugged. "I suppose I'll play it safe. That's the best answer for me, and the best for the missing girls. There's no time for yet another layer of weirdness within the task force, and there'll be no time for it afterward, because Tucker will be gone in a week or so."

And though that was the best plan, the safest plan, it didn't settle well in her gut, which churned with desire, and it didn't ring true with the little voice deep in her soul that whispered, *What harm could it do if both of you know it's only a one-time thing? Only temporary?*

She wished the temptation away and said, "I'm going to head upstairs and work on reassembling as much of the lost data as I can. Thanks for trying, anyway. I owe you one."

She turned for the doorway and stepped past a series of scuff marks carved in the dust and ash left by the bomb blast. The scene had already been photographed, but she automatically skirted around the area, keeping to the tracks left by the bomb squad.

Then she froze, stunned. Tracks!

She must have gasped aloud, because Maya said, "What is it? You've got something?"

"Feet!" Alissa said excitedly. She pointed down at the tracks in the white-gray ash. "Not feet, but footprints. I saw footprints in the snow tunnel when I went in after Lizzie!"

And if she could reproduce them, or even better find what was left of them…

…the Forensics Division would have something to work with.

Chapter Ten

Tucker's gut told him the answer even before the radio
report came through. Ferguson had given them the slip.
He'd been at the Shady Lady Motel—fingerprints
proved it—but he was long since gone. Had the credit
card purchase been a decoy? A taunt? A warning?

Tucker didn't know, and he hated the feeling of im-
potence, of being one step removed from the main
action. That was why he didn't work with partners—he
didn't want to be responsible for another person. If it
weren't for Alissa, he'd be out at the motel, questioning witnesses.

Hell, if it weren't for Alissa, he'd be in Rock Creek.

And where had that thought come from? His delay
had nothing to do with her and everything to do with
the case. The task force. Heck, until a couple of days
earlier, she'd been nothing more to him than an annoyance.

Right?

Irritated with himself, with the situation, he scowled

and grabbed his coat off the back of his chair. The air in the PD had cleared enough that they'd shut the windows, but he was still chilled, deep down inside. He told himself it was because the case refused to gel, but he feared it had more to do with the phone call and his promise to Whitethorne.

He had two days to find the kidnapper and make sure the bastard never touched Alissa again. Two days to avoid getting in any deeper with her than he already was.

A noise from the basement stairs alerted him a half second before she appeared, pink-cheeked and flustered, with excitement riding high in her eyes and a loaded duffel bag over her shoulder. She called across the room, "Come on! We need to get to the state forest right now!"

The roomful of cops silenced until Tucker thought he could have heard a spent casing drop two buildings away. A single snicker broke the quiet. Irritation spiked quickly in his gut, but before he could react, Alissa spun and shot Piedmont a filthy look, then widened it to include the others. "Grow up, all of you. You don't have to like me, but stop wasting my time. I have a kidnapper to catch." She spun and stalked out the door, calling over her shoulder, "With me, Tucker."

The others looked at him, probably expecting him to blow up or blow her off. Instead he nodded and shrugged his jacket over his shoulder holster. "You heard her. We've got work to do."

There wasn't a peep behind him when he stalked

out, which was lucky for them, as he was long past being out of patience with the internal garbage at the BCCPD.

Alissa had already climbed into the SUV. Part of him was surprised she hadn't insisted on driving. That same part of him was surprised to realize he would have let her.

Instead he hitched himself into the driver's seat and started the engine. "Where to?"

"The site where Lizzie was dumped." She stared straight ahead, lips pressed together in a firm line. "Maya helped me remember that when I went in after her, I stayed to the left side because I wanted to avoid the footprints."

Hope flared in Tucker's gut, then died just as quickly. "Prints would have been destroyed in the blast, or by the excavation afterward. The bomb techs were looking for fragments of the device or other evidence. Not for footprint shadows."

"I know." She glanced at him, blue eyes dark in her pale, determined face. "But I have to make sure. If we can lift even a portion of a print…"

He nodded. "Yeah. It could give us our connection between Lizzie and Ferguson. Maybe even enough leverage to convince him to give up the other girls when we catch him." But the conviction in his voice rang hollow. He took a breath. "About Ferguson." He saw Alissa stiffen in her seat and hated that he didn't have better news. "He's definitely in the area. He checked into a motel on the other side of the mountain this morning but buggered off before we got there." He paused to acknowledge the hollow worry in his chest. "That pretty much seals it. He's here, and he's looking for you." Looking to hurt her.

Alissa took a breath and then nodded, as though schooling herself not to react. But when she glanced over at him, her eyes were dark with worry. "Then I guess I'll have to trust you to watch my back, won't I?"

"Yeah," he agreed, hating that he felt all churned up about it, wishing it were that simple. "I guess you will."

The rest of the ride passed in silence.

By the time they pulled off the main state park road and bumped toward Bear Claw Canyon, the cold winter sun had edged toward the treetops, and the temperature had dropped a good five degrees. The wind had freshened, and the combination was enough to chill Tucker when he climbed from the SUV.

He didn't fasten his jacket, though. He wanted to be able to get at his weapon if he needed to. He cursed the itch in his gut, the heat on the back of his neck that warned of watching eyes. Maybe it was the kidnapper, maybe it was wild animals, maybe it was the power of suggestion. Whatever the cause, he stayed close to Alissa's side as she climbed out of the vehicle.

He gestured at the duffel. "Want me to carry that?"

"No, thanks. Keep your hands free, just in case." Her words and her serious, blue-eyed look told him that she felt it too, the sense of being watched.

Of being stalked.

The snowfall of the night before had covered over the

old tracks, leaving the area beside the canyon looking fresh and innocent, as though nothing bad could happen there. Even the deep scar that had once been an ice tunnel was little more than a white-shrouded depression that took on jagged definition once they walked closer.

"I'll stay up here and keep watch while you work," Tucker said, his words emerging on a puff of frosty white vapor.

"Come down in the canyon with me," she countered. "Making yourself a target won't help."

He frowned. "I'm a lookout, not a target." But he joined her in the partially excavated trench. "Can I help?"

The sooner they found—or didn't find—evidence of the footprints, the sooner they could leave the park and get her someplace safe. The cop in him wanted to stay there until the light gave out, but the man in him wanted her somewhere safe, far away from the canyon and its grisly memories.

"You take that side," she said, interrupting his thoughts with a tossed flashlight. "Stay near the edge of the tunnel and keep your feet near the middle, where the cops have walked."

He did as he was told, focusing half his attention on the snow and the other half on their surroundings. The sense of being watched had faded somewhat, likely because they were out of the open, but he let his jacket hang open just in case.

Anyone aiming for Alissa would have to go through him to get her. And that was both the cop and the man talking.

"See anything?" he said quietly.

"Nothing," she replied in the same low tones. Their hushed voices added to the cathedral feeling of the canyon, intensifying the feeling of dead spaces and cold, lonely graves. Tucker shook off a sudden chill as she continued, "I can discount the prints on top of the cave-in right away, and since there were only a few bomb techs allowed down here for evidence collection, I should be able to subtract their prints. Which leaves me looking for an icicle in a snow bank. Not impossible to find, but not easy, either."

"Gotcha." Tucker worked his side of the crevice in tandem with her, shining his light into the tricky, icy angles created by the fallen tunnel. Several times the indirect light caught a likely crease in the snow, but each time, closer inspection revealed just another ice lump, or a chunk of blasted rock.

Hell, for all he knew, he'd already walked past a perfect footprint filled with ice from above, or smeared beneath a layer of soot. The frustration of it nagged at him alongside wariness as the sun dipped well below the tree line and the quick winter dusk approached.

Having seen no evidence that they were being watched or stalked, Tucker decided to risk a quiet conversation to relieve the monotony of the search. "How'd you decide on crime-scene analysis?"

She glanced over at him. "Don't you mean why do I do a job that's so bloody tedious, that no real cop in his or her right mind would ever consider specializing in?" Her volume climbed. "Don't you mean to ask if I ever wish I'd decided to be a real cop, one who—"

Irritated in an instant, Tucker crossed the narrow gully and grabbed her arm. "Keep your voice down. And, no, that wasn't what I asked or what I meant." Though maybe it had been. That didn't change the fact that his blood hummed at the feel of her arm beneath his hand, even through heavy winter clothing.

She had frozen at his touch. Now she turned and looked up at him, eyes shaded with resentment and something else, something hotter and more volatile. Maybe anger. Maybe passion. "I know you're a gut-instinct cop who sometimes looks before he leaps. Exactly the kind that makes my life more difficult, because then I'm expected to tidy up the mess you've left of the evidence. You want to know why I picked crime-scene analysis? Because someone had to, and because I'm good at it."

The simple statement was all the answer he'd been looking for in the first place, but it didn't blunt his spiky temper. He tightened his grip on her arm. "I've never asked you to clean up a crime-scene mess."

His voice was low, dangerous, but she didn't flinch, didn't back down. Instead her eyes darkened and she hissed, "Only because you won't be here long enough to make one."

Then the brittle facade cracked just a little, and he saw the vulnerability beneath. The truth punched him beneath the heart. They weren't fighting about their jobs. They were fighting about the relationship they'd decided not to have.

"Alissa," he said quietly. "I told you before, I—"

"Don't bother repeating yourself, McDermott. We're

both intelligent people. You're not a long-term guy. I get that. But I'll admit that I'm having a hard time remembering why that's a bad thing."

The very air around them stilled. Tucker froze in place, with his hand on her arm. "What are you saying?"

The sky seemed to darken a degree around them, pushing them together and insulating them from the outside world. She swayed toward him, or maybe he leaned down to her. Whichever of them moved first, the change put her lips within range of his when she said, "I'm saying maybe we should enjoy each other while it's convenient and part friends when it isn't anymore."

Lust jolted through Tucker at the invitation, one he'd been only too happy to accept too many times before. It was his ideal relationship—no strings, no commitments, no misunderstandings…

At least on the surface. But he couldn't help thinking that this wasn't Alissa's style.

He drew back and looked into her eyes, but saw only awareness. Temptation. Nervous daring. She wasn't sure of herself, but it was clear she knew exactly what she was offering.

And to whom.

He reached down and touched her cold-stung lips with his fingertips when he would have rather kissed her until they were both senseless. "Bad idea."

Her eyes flashed with anger or maybe amusement. "It's the perfect idea and you know it." She shrugged as if it didn't matter, though the tension in her body told him that it mattered too much. "I'll be headed home after this. I assume you're coming with me, given that you're on bodyguard detail. I'll make us dinner. After that…well, it's up to you." She turned away with a cocky toss of her head that was ruined by the faint, vulnerable stain of a blush.

She worked her way back to the edge of the crevice and focused her light on the edges. He wanted to call her back. He wanted her to go and stop confusing him.

Hell, he didn't know what he wanted anymore, and that was damned dangerous.

So instead of following her and demanding the explanation his brain needed, or the kiss his body needed, he turned back to his own side and stared down at the snow.

And saw the footprint.

ALISSA WAS STARING blankly at a chunk of dirty ice, face flaming, wondering what the hell she'd just done, when she heard Tucker's hiss. She turned toward him, barely daring to hope. "You find something?"

"Maybe. You'd better have a look."

Layers of protocol and procedure slipped over her shoulders, and she was wholly focused on the job when she nudged his big body aside to see what he had found. He directed the yellow beam of his hand light toward the crevice wall, where a wide, flat chunk of ice had broken off in the explosion. A latticework of roots was mixed with the dirty snow, and had formed a hinge near the canyon wall. One edge of the ice sheet touched the frozen canyon floor, while the other hung suspended, forming a sort of shelter over a small section of the original tunnel floor.

"Good. Looks good," she said more to herself than to him. She shone her light obliquely behind the tilted shelf of ice and saw the shadows that had caught Tucker's attention. It sure looked like a footprint. And in that position, it seemed unlikely it could have come from one of the other evidence techs.

A frisson of excitement shimmered up her spine as she dug in her duffel for her camera and notebook. She pulled off her gloves, jammed them in her pocket and passed the notebook to Tucker. "Flip to the paper clipped page and take notes, will you? We'll use the microcorder, as well."

Though the brain of her camera would record each f-stop and distance, she would keep a manual log of the crime scene, as well. Some might call it paranoid. She called it thorough.

Without comment he flipped to the proper page and stood there, pencil poised, awaiting her words. The setting sun cast him in stark relief, a dark, manly silhouette against a salmon-colored sky.

She focused on the footprint. She stated the date, then said, "Possible footprint at first blast site approximately where Officer Wyatt remembers seeing footprints in tunnel prior to explosion."

She worked the scene, reporting her observations and trusting him to catch her words. She photographed the ice and footprint in situ before dragging her gloves back over her frozen fingertips and digging in the duffel for a pair of handheld shears. "Time to get this out of the way and see what we've got."

"Let me." Tucker took the tool and edged her aside, but she couldn't resent his interference when he cut the roots free and lifted the slab of ice away in one smooth, muscle-bunching motion that brought a sizzle that had very little do to with the uncovered evidence and everything to do with the man himself.

With the promise of what might happen later.

Focus! she told herself, simultaneously loving and hating the nervous, excited jangle in her stomach. Then she really did focus, and what she saw nearly doubled the excited jangle.

A perfect, pristine bootprint.

She hissed in triumph, but was quick to say aloud, "It might not be his. It could've been one of the evidence tech's, and the ice fell over it later as the scene settled. Heck, it could be my footprint from when I duck-walked in there." A memory that still brought a shiver of nerves, and the smell of earth and fear.

"But you don't think so," Tucker said quietly, reassuring her without even knowing it.

"No. I don't." She stood on one foot and held hers off to the side of the print for comparison. "Too big to be mine."

"Looks like a man's print." Tucker crowded close behind her. "See any identifying marks on the sole?"

Alissa shook her head and angled the yellow flashlight beam, which seemed stronger now as the sun set behind them. "Can't really tell. We'll be able to see it better once I've done the cast."

She photographed the footprint with and without a

ruler lying beside it for perspective. Then she passed the camera over. "Take a few frames while I'm doing this. It never hurts to have extra pictures."

She tried not to notice the flash as she prepared her work site. She shook the aerosol can of snow wax, then sprayed the first layer onto the footprint. The wax emerged blood red, turning the print into a gory splash.

The effect had always mildly creeped her out, but this time was worse than usual, making her think of what might have happened if she'd been a little later to find Lizzie, or if Tucker and the others had been a little slower to dig down through all that heavy, shifting weight.

When the memory of it threatened to press against her lungs, she forced herself to breathe and lay another coat of wax. She spoke to Tucker, aware of him at her back. "I use dental mold plaster because it's got the finest grain. Catches more details. But it's exothermic— generates heat as it sets. Between that and the weight, you can't pour straight into a snow footprint, so I use the snow wax first to stabilize the print. It's red so the details show up better under white light."

That was the only reason for the color, she knew, but still she wished they manufacturers had chosen something else. A cool blue, maybe, or a lush, verdant green.

Anything but blood red, the color of violence, of explosions and pain.

Something touched her shoulder and she nearly jumped out of her skin.

"Easy there," Tucker's voice said. "It's me. Are you okay?"

Her face flamed as she realized she was crouched down over the half-waxed footprint, nearly paralyzed with the cold. Reflexively she sprayed another layer of wax. "Fine. I'm fine."

"Good, because I don't mean to rush you, but we're running out of daylight and we'll make good targets in the dark."

"Right. One more coat of wax, then the dental mortar." Alissa forced herself to focus on that moment, on the motions of her hands and the protocol of snow casting. "You can start mixing if you want. One bottle of water goes into the zipper baggie of mortar. I pre-measured everything."

"Efficient," he commented.

"I try." She sprayed the final layer of blood-red wax and waited a minute for it to dry, then gestured for the plaster. "I'll take that. Can you grab the Popsicle sticks out of my duffel?"

He did as she asked while she gently emptied the mortar into the stabilized footprint. When she took the sticks, their fingertips brushed, leaving a warning buzz behind.

She made the mistake of glancing up and found herself trapped in his dark eyes. A shudder started deep within her, but she clamped it down ruthlessly, knowing it was neither the time nor the place for the desire that never quite seemed to die down between them.

Apparently he agreed, because instead of commenting, he said, "Fitz used leaves and twigs to strengthen his plaster casts."

"Well I use Popsicle sticks. Consider it a modern innovation." She arranged all but one of the narrow wooden strips across the print and tapped them into the tacky plaster. Then she used the remaining stick to scratch her name, the date and the case number into the nearly set surface.

"Ready?" Tucker asked, his voice muffled by a quick, cold gust of wind.

"Nearly." She held out her hand. "I'll take the camera back." She snapped a few more frames, just to be on the safe side.

All the *i*'s dotted and the *t*'s crossed. She wasn't leaving any wiggle room for the bastard. If they caught him—no *when*, she told herself—when they caught him, she didn't want any lawyer getting him off on a technicality.

Not this time.

And as though the thought had brought it crashing down around them, night fell with grim finality. The world went from dusky red to black in an instant, and the temperature dropped a good ten degrees. Alissa glanced up into the yellow glow of his flashlight. "Whoa. That was quick."

"Squall's coming," Tucker answered. He touched her arm, then took the now-empty plastic bag from her. "You finished?"

"I guess I'll have to be." Hurrying now with the storm wind at her back, she eased the cast out of the footprint and wrapped it for transport in her duffel. "Can you lay the ice slab back over the footprint for me? Just in case."

He did as she asked then reached down and slung the duffel strap over his shoulder. He held out a gloved hand. "Come on. We've really got to get out of here."

That was when she saw it in his eyes. Not just fear for the storm. Something else.

She let him draw her to her feet, and her heart kicked up a notch when the first small, grainy snowflake landed on her face, heralding the incoming storm. She held out a hand for the duffel. "Let me carry it."

He nodded shortly and handed over the bag, confirming her half-formed suspicion. "Douse your light. It makes too clear a target."

She didn't ask whether he'd seen or heard someone. His instincts were enough for her, which was a surprise. Since when did she trust anyone else's instincts over her own rational, scientific investigation?

She didn't, she told herself. She couldn't. But she snapped her light off, and the yellow beam gave way to the eerie blue-black of snow and night. She slung the duffel strap crosswise over her shoulder and clamped the bag—and its precious contents—beneath her arm. "Ready."

He muttered something unintelligible, but then his voice sharpened. "Let's go."

In the strange light of the storm, she saw him draw his weapon, which was obscurely comforting and unsettling at the same time.

They worked their way into the main canyon, and from there up toward where they'd left the SUV. Their tracks were clearly visible in the old snow, not yet covered by the new flakes, which fell with increasing intensity.

"No new tracks," Alissa said quietly.

"Doesn't mean he's not out there." Tucker drew her closer to his left side, where he could cover her but keep his gun hand free. "Let's hustle."

They jogged to the SUV and checked it over—no new tracks, no sign of tampering. No block-lettered note. But still, it wasn't until they were locked inside and driving down the road that either of them relaxed, ever so slightly.

Finally Alissa blew out a breath. "Phew. Think we talked ourselves into having a case of the creeps?" Her fingers ached with the strength of her grip on the duffel and their newest clue.

A footprint wasn't as good as a fingerprint, but it was a start.

Tucker tapped the brakes and turned onto the main road, away from the state forest. He slid a glance in her direction. "Would it make you feel better if I said we had?"

"Not if you didn't mean it."

"Then there's your answer." He returned his attention to the road, which was just slick enough with the icy snow to present a challenge. He eased off on the gas and popped the SUV into four-wheel drive as the road wound along the edge of Bear Creek Canyon. "He was out there. I'm sure of it."

But not sure enough to radio it in and drop a net around the park, she noted. Or else he'd been so intent on getting her away that he'd opted against setting a trap, which made no sense. They were both cops, weren't they?

Cops and perhaps something more, she knew. Their earlier conversation hummed beneath her skin like an interrupted aria, buoyant and waiting. She turned to him. "Listen, Tucker. I think—"

An engine revved and bright high-beams splashed light into the cab of the SUV, coming from a truck bigger and faster than theirs, too close behind, approaching too fast.

Tucker cursed. "Where did he come from?"

But they both knew. The truck had been running dark, unnoticed in the blue-black dusk and the falling snow, sneaking up on them until it was too late.

Until there was no escape.

"Get us out of here!" Alissa snapped, heart lodged in her throat. The SUV's headlights gleamed on the metal guardrail, which was all that separated them from Bear Creek Canyon. The chasm wasn't terribly deep at this edge of the state park—

But it was deep enough.

"Hang on!" Tucker hit the gas hard enough to send them forward, not enough to send them spinning on the snow-slicked road. His knuckles had gone white on the steering wheel and his jaw was set in an implacable line.

Alissa grabbed the roll bar handle with one hand and scrambled for the in-dash radio with the other. A mad, desperate plan began to form in her head. "You drive and I'll call it in. If we can keep ahead of him long enough for the others to reach us…"

Tucker didn't even glance over. "Big *if,* babe."

Then it wasn't even an *if,* because the truck closed in and rammed them from behind. Alissa screamed as the SUV jolted forward, then yawed to one side.

Tucker cursed and fought the wheel. The back end of the SUV broke loose and skidded directly toward the guardrail—and the emptiness beyond.

Chapter Eleven

Tucker cursed and steered into the skid, wrestling with the wheel as all four tires fought for purchase on the slick road. The SUV whipped side to side and then steadied, but it was too late. They slammed into the metal guardrail with a crash and the scream of metal on metal.

But the railing held. The SUV kept going.

Heart thundering over the engine's roar, Tucker bullied the vehicle into the center of the road and hit the gas. "Hang on. I'm getting us out of here!"

"You drive." Alissa's voice was sharp with stress. "I'll buy us some time."

Tucker glanced over at her. The light from too-close headlights sliced into the cab and threw her profile into sharp relief as she dug into her duffel and pulled out a service weapon in a holster so new it creaked when she unsnapped it and pulled the gun free.

The truck behind them wound its engine to near blow-out levels and rammed the SUV with a sickening crunch. The jolt snapped Tucker's head back against the seat. He recovered quickly, muscled the SUV back into the middle of the road, and said a quick thanks that they were nearly to the down hill, where the canyon fell away from the road and they might be able to gain some ground.

The wind roared louder and he looked over in time to see Alissa buzz down her window and loosen her seat belt so she could spin around to face backward.

Tucker's heart jammed in his throat when she shimmied halfway out of the speeding vehicle. He shouted, "What the hell are you doing?" He reached over and grabbed the back of her parka. "Get back in here! Do you even know how to use that thing?"

"Well enough," she called back over her shoulder. "I just want to get him off our tail a—"

Whump! The truck plowed into the rear of the SUV with more force this time, and Alissa screamed as she was banged around in the open window. The force of the blow knocked the steering wheel from Tucker's hand and sent the SUV spinning.

"Alissa! Get the hell back in here!" Cursing, he let go of her jacket, grabbed the wheel and fought the SUV back on course. Snow spewed beneath the tires and coated the windshield, making it nearly impossible for him to tell which way was front anymore. "Alissa!"

His only answer was a trio of gunshots.

"I got him," she shouted. "I see him. It's Ferguson! I—"

The other truck spun into white-hazed motion,

swerving across the road and slamming into the guard-rail. The back end exploded upward and the truck flipped end over end—

Directly over the guardrail.

Alissa screamed, but the sound was quickly swamped by a crash of brush and a howl of metal as the other vehicle smashed down into the canyon.

Damn it! Tucker fought the SUV to a slithering stop, then slapped the transmission into Reverse. The tires wouldn't bite. He lost valuable time seesawing them until he could get the vehicle turned around and slogging back uphill. He slid to a stop near the bent section of guardrail, then killed the engine.

In the snow-deadened distance, he could hear the sob of sirens. Backup was on its way, but would likely be too late.

Alissa unhooked her belt and bolted from the SUV. Tucker called in a priority request for an ambulance, though he had little hope they would need one.

That'd been a hell of a crash.

He grabbed their flashlights and quickly joined Alissa at the edge of the road, where she stood huddled inside her jacket, shaking with the cold and probably shock.

She still clutched her gun.

"I'll take that." He slipped the weapon from her fingers, checked it and tucked it in his pocket. "You okay?"

"We should get down there," she said, not really an-swering his question. But she was steady as she worked her way along the road, so she could slither down the canyon embankment at a distance from the actual crash site and preserve the evidence. Though procedure dictated that he wait up on the road, both to brief the incoming cops and to keep extra tracks off the crime scene, Tucker damned protocol and followed.

No way he was letting her down there alone. There was no telling what Ferguson might do if he was conscious.

If he was alive. The thought brought a knot to Tucker's gut. Under any other circumstance, he wouldn't have cared. Serial rapists were better off dead than alive in his book. But these weren't just any circumstances.

Alissa's bobbing flashlight reached the bottom of the canyon, some twenty feet below the road. As elsewhere, Bear Claw Canyon wasn't deep, but it made up for its shallowness with irregularity. She was nearly lost to his view behind a fan of scrub brush, and the falling snow, but his flashlight beam glinted off her outline, and the tense set of her shoulders.

"He'd better be alive." Her soft voice carried to him. "If he's not…" She trailed off, but they both knew the alternative. If Ferguson was dead, they could be stuck trying to backtrack his movements over the past weeks to find the missing girls.

Like finding an ice cube in a glacier field.

It seemed like the lives of Maria Blackhorse and Holly Barrett hung in the balance, capable of tipping either way based on what they found in the wrecked truck. The vehicle lay on its side, the only hint of motion coming from a wheel spinning in ever-slowing revolutions, cast in the bloody red of broken taillights.

"Hey," he said. "You did what you had to do. We'll deal with the consequences."

She squared her shoulders beneath her parka. "I know."

They approached the vehicle warily, careful not to disturb any of the accident debris. She photographed everything twice, working quickly as the hard, icy pellets of snow raced her for the scene.

Just before they reached the truck, a voice hailed them from above. "You need the paramedics down there?"

Tucker directed his flashlight beam up to the road. The figure at the edge of the guardrail was snow-shrouded and indistinct, but the voice was Chief Parry's. Tucker cupped his hands around his mouth and called into the storm, "We're okay, Chief. We're checking on the vic right now."

Though, calling the bastard a victim seemed inappropriate. At the very least, he was guilty of assaulting two police officers with his one-ton pickup. At the worst, he was a rapist, a kidnapper and a murderer.

Scowling, Tucker turned toward the truck and saw that Alissa was there ahead of him, her fingers at the throat of a slack-faced man whose dark hair was wet with blowing snow and blood. She turned back, eyes dark with an indefinable emotion. "He's dead."

Tucker cursed, not from regret or remorse, but from the knowledge that the death would complicate more than it solved. He took a longer look in the harsh beam of the high-powered flashlight. The man's face was busted up some, testimony to the plunge and the star-shaped impact site on the windshield. "He wasn't wearing his seat belt."

"No, he wasn't," Alissa agreed, her voice faltering on the rising storm wind. "And yes, it's Ferguson." She jammed her hands in her pockets. "Damn it." She turned away and scuffed at the piling snow with the toe of her boot. "I shouldn't have shot out his tire. We were almost to level ground. You could've outrun him, or at least stayed ahead of him until the others closed in. Now we've got nothing. My fault."

"No. There's no guarantee we would have made it to level ground." He touched her hand and imagined the warmth of flesh beneath the layers of clothing. "You did good. Now let's work your scene." He hunched his shoulders beneath his leather jacket. "I'm betting we'll find something useful in the truck."

She turned her full attention on him, seeming oblivious of the other cops now working their way down into the canyon and the tow truck backing into the broken gap of guardrail. "What aren't you telling me?"

"I'm not sure. Something…" Tucker glanced at the still figure in the truck. "Something doesn't feel right about this."

He expected her to snarl at his instincts. Instead, her eyes darkened. "I know what you mean."

Those five soft words chilled him to the bone, and he thought, *Hell, now what?*

Because if Alissa was ready to go with her instincts, they must be in worse trouble than he'd thought.

Suddenly, inexplicably, he felt the fine hairs on the back of his neck prickle as though someone was watching. Someone other than the cops on the road above. But that made no sense. Their suspect was dead.

Wasn't he?

Half convinced he was losing it, Tucker edged his body between her and the feeling of being watched. A feeble anger burned in his chest, alongside his frustration for the kidnapped girls, and he felt a low-grade sense of shame that he'd agreed to move on to Rock Creek in under forty-eight hours and hadn't yet told Alissa.

Hell, he thought, on a spurt of aggravation. Why did he have to tell her anything? He'd clearly spelled out the boundaries. Regardless of the attraction, he didn't owe her an explanation. He was simply acting true to form, true to his nature. He had no reason to feel ashamed of it.

Aware that he'd nearly talked himself into an anger entirely of his own making, he turned away from her and nodded as Chief Parry joined them near the truck. "Chief." He gestured at the crash and the dead man. "Guess we've got some work to do."

Parry nodded, including Alissa in the gesture. "Guess we do." Then he gestured the others forward. "Come on, people. Work it by the book. We've got a long night ahead of us."

And it was only just beginning.

THE CRASH SITE wasn't cleared until nearly 3:00 a.m. By that time, Alissa's body had shut down and she was running on adrenaline and nerves. Adrenaline from the chase, the crash and the investigation. Nerves because the evidence wasn't lining up the way she wanted it to. The way she *needed* it to.

Once the body had been removed for further examination, she and Cassie had gone over the truck carefully, though they would repeat the process once the wreck was hauled into the BCCPD lot. They had found clues aplenty—Ferguson wasn't any more careful now than he had been before. The litter of crumpled receipts clearly sketched his journey. That was the good news.

The bad news was that if the receipts could be believed, he'd been at a gas station, purchasing fuel and food, at the time of Lizzie's kidnapping.

Damn it, Alissa thought, then realized she'd said the words aloud when Tucker appeared at her shoulder and asked, "Problem?"

"Just a few," she muttered, going for professionalism when she wanted to grab on to him and shout her frustrations. "The footprint we lifted from the ice tunnel doesn't match the boots Ferguson was wearing."

"He could've stashed stuff at another motel."

"True," she agreed, "but he wears a size ten. Unless he pulled on a pair of twelves to confuse us just in case he left tracks, those weren't his prints."

"We've done what we can for the moment," Cassie said from behind them.

Alissa glanced at her and nodded. "Fine. We'll follow you back to the station. Does Varitek have the mobile unit on site yet? We can—"

"Turn it off for a few hours," Tucker said firmly. He clamped a hand on Alissa's arm and turned her toward the place where a knotted rope had been tied to the guardrail as an aid for cops climbing up and down the canyon wall. "You haven't slept in nearly twenty-four hours. You're done."

She bristled at his tone. "You've been up as long as I have, McDermott."

"Exactly. I'm done, too. We both need some rest or we'll be no good to anyone." He boosted her up the canyon wall, leaving her no choice but to grab for the rope and pull herself the rest of the way up.

When they reached the SUV, she jammed her hands in her pockets. "I'd rather go to the station with Cassie, if you don't mind."

"I do mind." Tucker opened the passenger door for her, a touch of chivalry she'd gotten unwisely accustomed to. "Get in." When she balked, he blew out a frustrated breath. "Teamwork, remember? Let the others do their jobs."

Cassie nodded. "I'll run your footprint cast myself." She sent a dark look back at her pickup truck, where a large silhouette was visible in the passenger seat. "I don't like Mr. FBI, but he's proving useful. He'll get us into the big databases more quickly than I can manage. We'll have a brand and distributor on that boot by morning."

"Hopefully we won't need them," Alissa said, though hope was the last thing she was feeling at that moment. "If we're lucky we'll be able to backtrack Ferguson's travels and find the girls."

But her gut told her otherwise. And from the look in Cassie's eyes, she held little hope of it being that easy. Hell, the receipts in Ferguson's truck all but gave him a post-mortem alibi.

He might have come to Bear Claw looking to hurt her, but he hadn't set the bombs and he hadn't taken the girls.

Which left them where? Frustration rose in Alissa's chest, alongside the desire to kick something. Unexpectedly, tears prickled in her eyes. She swiped at them and told herself she wasn't weak, she was just tired.

Cassie saw, and nudged her toward the SUV. "Go on. I'll call if anything breaks."

Alissa sniffled and felt miserably tired. "Promise?"

"I promise. Now go."

She went, but she didn't like the knot in her stomach as Tucker shut the door after her, and she didn't like the press of tears. What was the matter with her? Of the three women in the Forensics Department, she was the pragmatic one, the one who could keep even the most stressful cases in perspective. She prided herself on not letting the fear get to her, not bringing the evil home once it was time to call it a day.

But this case was different. *She* was different.

She stared out the foggy window for the duration of the short drive to her house, grateful that Tucker didn't insist on a conversation. It felt like they'd already said too much in the past few days. Instead of relaxing when they pulled into her driveway, she felt even tenser.

She glanced over at him as she unlocked the front door. He had his coat open, for easy access to his weapon, and a look of haunted intensity on his face that made her wonder whether he was thinking about Ferguson and the missing girls.

"I'll look around," he said abruptly, and brushed past her into the house.

"You do that." She closed the door behind him, but kept her hand on the cool wood a beat too long as part of her wished she could climb into her VW and drive somewhere else, anywhere else that she could put aside her work and her emotions for an hour or two. But she couldn't. It wasn't safe for her out there.

Unfortunately, it didn't feel particularly safe for her inside, either, though for very different reasons. Tucker's presence beat just beneath her skin, in time with the rush of blood through her body.

Knowing she could either face him or avoid him, she locked the front door and turned toward Tucker when he emerged from her bedroom, expression closed. They stared at each other for a heartbeat. Then another, until the silence stretched thick between them, borne on the rising tension of being alone together.

Alissa cleared her throat and spoke first, forcing the words past her suddenly tight throat. "I…I guess I'll take a shower." She was cold and aching and dirty, but her words seemed to take on a sexual meaning the moment they were said.

Later they had said. They would follow up on those kisses later.

Well, later was now.

Tucker's eyes darkened, and he inhaled a deep breath. The motion stretched his broad shoulders even wider, until he seemed to fill the doorway with his wild, untamed presence. She thought he might offer to join her, or say something, anything that would lead them to the discussion they both knew was inevitable.

But instead, he stepped aside wordlessly and gestured her through. When she didn't move, he turned for the kitchen. "I'll put together something for…whatever meal we missed."

I'm not hungry for food, she thought out of nowhere, but didn't set the words free. It was near four in the morning, and lunch was a fond memory. They needed food and sleep in that order, so they would be ready to go the next day, ready to find the missing girls and the kidnapper she was nearly sure was still at large.

But her body wasn't revving for food or sleep. It was revving for Tucker.

And what the hell was she going to do about that?

Nothing, she decided. Absolutely nothing. So she marched past him, through her bedroom and into the bath.

She banged the door behind her, not even sure why she was suddenly furious.

THE DOOR SLAM cracked like a shot, echoing the snap and roil inside Tucker. He set his teeth and opened the refrigerator, hoping for something quick and easy. They needed to eat and crash before either of them did something stupid.

Hell, before they *both* did something stupid. Together.

He pulled out ingredients at random, all too aware when the shower kicked on. He forced himself not to imagine her naked, forced himself not to picture the slick slide of soap, the glistening pink of skin. But he wasn't able to short-circuit the memory of her taste.

"I'm leaving," he said to himself as he slapped bread onto plates with unnecessary force. "Day after tomorrow I'll be in the wind."

He cursed when the thought brought little pleasure, then cursed again when he realized he hadn't even taken his jacket off. He stripped out of the leather bomber and tossed it over the arm of her plush sofa, out in the living room. Then he stood in the center of the warm, inviting space and looked around.

The knickknacks were few and far between, the pictures even fewer. An end table held a framed shot of Alissa with an older, more somber version of herself, taken at her graduation from the academy. Her mother, most likely. Beside it rested a candid photo of Alissa, Cassie and Maya, taken somewhere warm and tropical looking. There was no picture of her father. The realization shouldn't have surprised Tucker, given the history there, but it did make him wonder whether she'd ever looked for the man.

Frowning, he returned to the kitchen and finished

making sandwiches. He took a bite to clear the memory of her sweet mouth from his tongue, but the food was tasteless in comparison. He couldn't remember the last time he'd been this caught up in a woman, and he didn't like it one bit.

"I'm leaving," he reminded himself aloud, and heard a small, startled sound from the doorway.

Oh, hell. He turned to find Alissa there, pale-blue eyes wide, blown-dry hair cascading over a fuzzy turquoise pullover. She wore faded jeans, warm socks and a dusky bruise over her cheek. The overall effect made her look too young. Too vulnerable. His throat locked and his feet stuck to the floor. What could he do? He couldn't go to her, didn't dare. Yet she pulled at him like a magnet. Like a compulsion.

She smiled sadly. "Don't look so guilty. You've never lied about leaving." She glanced at the sandwiches. "I'm not very hungry. I'm going to bed." She walked away, and he felt as though she took a piece of him with her. His chest was hollow, his stomach knotted, even though he knew this was the better answer, the kinder choice.

But then she stopped across the hall, in her bedroom doorway, and turned back to him. "You coming?"

His brain stalled. A hot wash of *Hell, yes* flared through his body and nearly left him reeling. But he held his ground.

"I won't be coming back once I go." He never did. Once he'd said goodbye to a place, there was no sense in revisiting old scenes. His mother had taught him that, when she'd cried over each old home, then dutifully packed up and made the next one her own. "This isn't a good time to start something."

"Correction." Her eyes kindled with something warm and welcoming, something that called to him. "It's the perfect time. No fuss, no muss, no surprise when it's over. Or can you honestly say that we'd be better off not finding out what it would be like?"

Tucker swallowed, his feet still glued in place. "That's exactly what I'm saying. If we don't start something, it doesn't have to end." His conscience clamored for him to tell her he was leaving in less than forty-eight hours. She deserved to know.

Didn't she?

"Seems to me like we've already started it," she said, and took a step inside the bedroom. "Now I'm thinking it's time to finish it, or we'll always be left wondering." Another step back. "Don't you wonder?"

"Hell, yes." But what if it was as good as he expected? What if it was the best? What if it was everything? He'd be tempted to stay and make it work, and then what would happen?

He'd get itchy like he always did, and they'd both pay the price for having given in to temptation.

Her eyes darkened and her lips turned down. She hugged her arms tighter across her body, as though reassuring herself, and he wished like hell he could hold her and explain the feelings he barely understood. He knew only that this was the better choice, the safer choice.

The only choice.

Slowly, she nodded. "Okay, if that's the way you want it. Offer's open for another few minutes if you want to think about it."

Then she shut the bedroom door between them, as much a challenge as a barrier.

"I don't need to think about it," he told himself. "I'm leaving. I'm leaving. I'm leaving."

He was still repeating the mantra again when his feet came unglued from the floor.

Chapter Twelve

Alissa's hands shook as she turned back the pretty, pale-green duvet she'd bought to match the high, stenciled border on the walls. She'd held it together well out there, she thought, but now that the moment was past, the question answered once and for all, she wasn't sure what she'd been thinking.

She hadn't been thinking at all. She'd been reacting. Dreaming.

"Stupid," she muttered to herself, and tugged at the waistband of her sweatshirt.

"Having second thoughts?"

At the sound of Tucker's voice, she spun with a gasp. He stood just inside the doorway, too large, too male for the feminine space. "What are you doing in here?"

He took another step inside the room, focusing her entire attention on the wide breadth of his shoulders and the open snap of his holster, which now hung loosely, ready to be shrugged free. "Is that invitation still open? Because if it is, I'd like to accept. You're right, knowing has to be better than wondering, no matter what happens after."

Though the words and the sentiment were hers, hearing them parroted back made them seem less sure, less logical. But then he closed the final distance between them and logic was lost.

She looked up at him and saw the steady pulse at his throat, faster than normal, beating in time with her heart. She inhaled, and his scent surrounded her, spicy and male, with the hint of wild woodlands in spring. Desire pooled in her midsection, sharp and sweet, and she nodded. "Yes. The invitation stands."

To hell with caution and history. She wanted this, and she was going into it with her eyes wide open. She could handle it, she told herself.

Knowing had to be better than wondering.

Still, even though she'd agreed, he stayed still, looking down at her with eyes that she only now admitted had haunted her, asleep or awake, for the months since she'd first seen him across a crowded dance floor. Realizing that he wanted her to make the first move, wanted her to be absolutely sure, she chucked caution to the wind and took the final step that brought them chest to chest.

His eyes darkened and his breath hitched ever so slightly. Emboldened by the thought that she affected him the way he did her, she lifted her hand and placed her palm on his warm, wide chest. She balanced there for a moment, equally able to draw him close and push him away, then curled her fingers into the material of his shirt and used the leverage to pull herself to tiptoe and align her mouth with his.

They kissed softly, chastely at first. The contact shimmered through her like the summer sun in winter, unexpected and powerful. She hummed her approval and pressed closer, but still he seemed to hold himself back, staying aloof from her even though he'd been the one to open the bedroom door.

She didn't know what doubts rode him, knew only that she was sure. So she kissed him once again, soothing rather than inciting, and said, "Kiss me like you mean it, like you did the night we first met." Like he'd kissed her before they knew each other at all.

"No," he murmured, and she felt him smile against her lips, felt some of the tension leave his big body. "I'll kiss you like I've wanted to every day since that first night."

As though the words had unlocked hidden floodgates of acceptance, he curled his powerful arms around her waist and boosted her up so their mouths were aligned and their eyes were level. He smiled, a rare, open expression, and the last lingering coil of insecurity, one she hadn't even known about until it was gone, melted within her, leaving her simultaneously boneless and invigorated.

Then he kissed her for real, and all other thoughts fled her brain. Heat slammed into her, blasted through her, leaving her limp and wanting, strong and needing.

His lips cruised over hers; his tongue sampled with maddeningly gentle caresses until she opened her mouth and demanded more.

He groaned her name and gave more.

Something hit the floor with a hollow thud. A dizzy part of her realized it was his holstered weapon, but the rest of her was focused on his mouth and his hands, which stroked downward, across her rib cage to possess and incite. Her nipples puckered to hard, wanting buds, and she moved restlessly against him, wordlessly demanding. When his next kiss soothed rather than blazed, she slid her hands beneath his shirt and went to work on his belt buckle.

A corner of her brain buzzed alarm that this was moving too fast, that she wasn't ready for this, wasn't ready for him, but she ignored it. Fast was the safer answer, the only answer. Their lovemaking—no, she corrected herself, not lovemaking but sex—their sex play needed to stay hot and edgy and tense, like the energy that had pulsed between them for the past few months. Hard and hot and fast.

Because if it didn't, if it tilted over the line to become slow and gentle, she knew she would be lost to him. If she wasn't already.

So she freed his belt and loosened his pants, then went to work on his shirt, the haze of excitement causing her to fumble while he slid her sweatshirt up and over her head, sending her hair free across her shoulders. His breath hissed out on an oath, or maybe her name when he saw that she was naked beneath. She remembered her nerves as she'd made the choice after her shower, both to come to him half-naked and to come to him at all. Now those nerves were gone, burned away with heat and sensation as they pressed together bare-chested.

They kissed harder now, giving her the speed and the sex she needed, pushing away weak thoughts of kindness and love. She slid her hands up his body, marveling at the hard, sculpted lines of his wide shoulders and taut, muscled arms. Then she tugged, and they fell back on her bed together, skin-to-skin above, separated by frustrating layers of material below.

They curled into each other, around each other with delicious friction that soothed some aches and created others. After a moment, or maybe an eon, Tucker lifted his head. His eyes were glazed and his rib cage heaved against hers, creating a delicious friction. "Do you have…" He made a vague gesture with his head. "Whatever?"

"Condom." She gestured and battled an unexpected flare of nerves. "Bedside table. A gift from Cassie and Maya." No need to tell him it was a symbolic "goodbye Aiden" gift the others had given her months earlier that she'd never had reason to unwrap. At least not until she'd stood in front of the bathroom mirror after her shower, nearly too nervous to walk into the kitchen, but equally sure that if she let this opportunity slip by, she'd regret it deeply.

He grinned. "I knew I liked those girls for a reason."

The absurdity surprised a snort out of her. "Baloney. You went out of your way to make us feel like complete outsiders because you were buddies with the sainted Fitz."

"Not true," he said. "I snubbed you because of what happened that night at the bar, and because it irritated me that I couldn't make myself forget the way you tasted, the way you felt in my arms. Beneath my fingertips." He punctuated his words with a slow slide of his hands up and down her body, then up again to link his fingers with hers in an unexpectedly tender gesture.

Alissa stiffened against a gentle wash of warmth, and her self-preservation instincts screamed, *Give me heat! Fast and hard! None of this mushy stuff!*

She liked it too damn much.

So she deliberately reached up and tangled her fingers in his hair. She used the leverage to tug his head down to hers and pour herself into a kiss designed to inflame him rather than bind them together. Then, as the electricity of connection arced between them, she feared she was already bound.

But it didn't matter, because the roar of heat rose up and swept her away on a tide of too much sensation. She was vaguely aware of struggling out of her jeans, of him doing the same, but her senses were focused on the touch of lips and tongue, the love play of a wild man's kiss.

McDermott, she thought, then, *Tucker.*

They rolled across the already rumpled bed together, and the world twirled around her, glittering colors shone behind her eyelids as she reveled in the smell and feel of him. This was what she had wanted, the heat and fire. But even as he stripped open a condom and sheathed himself, even as he rose above her, even as their eyes met, she feared she had been wrong, after all.

The gentleness wasn't a danger to her heart.

Tucker was.

He must have seen the flash of panic in her expression, because he paused above her at that last exquisite, anticipated moment. His eyes sought hers. "You okay?"

It touched her, deep inside, to know that even now, with their hearts thundering in time and their bodies on overdrive, he would stop if she wasn't sure. But though her brain had doubts, her body had none. Almost without conscious volition, she arched up and accepted him, welcomed him.

His eyes went stormy and he surged forward. Her cry of pleasure escaped as he filled her, completed her, touched a wanting bundle of nerves deep inside.

He dropped his head to her neck, and his hair feathered her face as he breathed a single word. "Alissa."

And then he began to move within her.

The desire for plunging heat and quick relief fled in that first instant, when the long slow glide of his flesh within her brought a thousand tiny fires to life, soothed a thousand tiny aches while inflaming others. Where before in Alissa's experience, sex had been a pleasant diversion or an added layer of intimacy, now it was so much more than that.

It was everything. *He* was everything.

She let her eyes fall shut. Her body moved with him and against him, an age-old rhythm laced with new excitement and overwhelming needs. She dug her fingers into his shoulders, into the warm, taut skin at his hips. He groaned, and excitement speared through her, arrowing from a point at the center of their joining, out to her too-sensitive fingertips.

She dragged her hands from his waist and let her fingernails scrape the skin over his ribs. He muttered restlessly and surged against her, speed building with no loss of the tenderness she feared. Wanting, needing the deeper connection, she opened herself fully to him, lifting her legs and wrapping them around his plunging hips. He paused for a moment, then drove into her, sheathing himself to the hilt and touching something deep within her.

A tidal wave of feeling slammed into her body, blasted through her until she might have thought she was blind except that she remembered closing her eyes. She clung to him, burrowing her fingers through his long hair when he turned his head to press his lips to her throat, her cheek, her mouth.

She poured herself into the kiss, allowing the maelstrom of sensation to strip her of all pretenses, all barriers. He whispered her name and thrust deep, and she felt all of him, big and male, surrounding her, filling her.

Her body tightened around him, fisting around his proud, hard flesh and wringing a groan from deep within his chest. The wash of feelings bounced back on her, overwhelming her. He thrust again, deeper, harder, until he touched her core and sent her spinning, exploding, flying on a detonation of greedy, pulsing flesh and orgasmic pleasure.

She bowed back against the sensations and opened

herself further, beyond what she thought her physical limits. He surged once more, still deeper, and set off another series of explosions within her as he groaned her name and stiffened.

His arms tightened around her, binding them together as he came. For the first time in her life, Alissa found herself wishing a condom away. She would have liked to feel his seed within her, would have liked to keep some part of him for herself.

At the thought, her heart stuttered and her insides fisted in a nervous parody of pleasure. Excitement drained, leaving her nervous and confused as their heartbeats began to slow, their bodies to cool.

Oh, hell.

She'd fallen for a guy who'd be gone in a couple of weeks.

TUCKER'S BRAIN hadn't fully clicked back online yet, but he was hyperaware of her body and knew the moment she tensed up. He wanted to beg her to relax for a few more minutes, but he knew her well enough not to bother. Instead he levered himself up onto his elbows so they were face-to-face, with him still cradled in the vee of her thighs, intimately connected.

"Regrets already? Want me to leave?" he asked, and found himself fervently hoping her answer would be no, on both counts. His brain hadn't yet gotten beyond the mind-shattering, blood-draining orgasm, but he instinctively knew things had shifted between them more than he'd expected. More than he'd wanted or intended.

He'd need to process that, and so would she. But he'd prefer to put it off until the morning. He was too damn comfortable to move, which set the warning bells jangling in the back of his brain.

Alissa's kiss-swollen lips tipped down at the corners, but she said, "No regrets and, no, I don't want you to leave. Unless you'd feel more comfortable on the couch?"

The shadows behind her eyes made it a loaded question. She might not outwardly blame him for wanting the distance, but it would reinforce her basic belief. Men left.

He shook his head and found a small smile. "I'd rather stay. I think we have unfinished business here."

He shifted onto one elbow so he could brush a strand of sweat-dampened hair from her cheek. Tenderness was an unfamiliar clutch in his chest. He tried to will it away, but it wouldn't stay gone. Instead the foreign emotion softened and slowed him when he leaned in to kiss her lips, her jaw, the side of her neck. It laid him bare when she stared up at him, eyes wary, and said, "Maybe this wasn't such a good idea."

"It's the perfect idea," he said, ignoring a slice of panic. He inhaled her warm, clean scent and felt himself harden again. "We deserve this break after what we've been through in the past few days. We need this. *I* need this."

He'd intended to keep it light, but that final, almost unwilling sentence derailed his plan, because it was the truth. He needed this. He needed *her.*

Half afraid she didn't need or want him with the same intensity, he poured himself into a kiss, and surged fully into her. It was a foolish, stupid risk not to don a fresh condom, but part of him worried that if he paused for that moment, the tension would snap back into her body and she would send him away. He wasn't ready for it to end. Not yet.

Not until morning.

So he shaped her body with his hands, inciting and soothing the flames between them. When he pulled away, he found her still watching him with those vulnerable, considering eyes, and he had to say, "Alissa?"

The single word encompassed so many questions he couldn't fully form. *Are you okay with this? Do you want me as much as I want you?*

And most confusing of all, *Do you know what comes next?*

Always before, the answer had been clear. They would go their separate ways and part friends, at best, irritated ex-lovers at worst, but without any of the complications and heartaches he'd worked so hard to avoid. But this time…

This time nothing was clear besides the beat of his heart and her final, welcoming smile when she softened and lifted her arms to link behind his neck. "Tucker."

Her answer wasn't an explanation, wasn't a promise. It was simply acceptance of what had happened between them, what would happen now.

Or so he hoped.

Refusing to think about it anymore, unable to think

past the thunder of blood through his body, Tucker surged inside her once more, fully hard now, fully wanting. When she murmured pleasure and tightened her fingers in the hair at his nape, he nearly gave in to the pounding urgency. But one last scrap of rationality prevailed, and he left her for the few moments necessary to dispose of the old condom and don fresh protection.

When he returned to her, she welcomed him with open arms and a long, drugging kiss, and when he slid into her again, that last scrap of rationality fled, and with it a fleeting thought.

What if he hadn't changed the condom? What if he hadn't used one at all? What if his seed caught in her womb, binding him to this woman, this place?

What if he was forced to stay put this time?

Then she moved beneath him, against him, fisting her hands in his hair, scraping her fingernails down the sensitive flesh across his ribs. His internal war fragmented into so many colored pieces and blasted him free of his own skin on a wash of pleasure and need and a stunning realization:

Maybe being tied to Alissa wouldn't be the end of the world, after all. Maybe she could be the one to hold him when the restlessness tried to drive him on.

Or maybe that was impossible.

IT WAS A SHORT NIGHT, made shorter by the number of times they turned to each other. They made love—for Alissa was done pretending that it was anything but helpless, hopeless love on her part—twice more; sometimes wordlessly, moving together as the moon broke through the storm clouds; sometimes with soft sounds and precious, meaningless wordplay as the fat moon faded toward dawn.

In between those times she slept fitfully, waking what seemed like a thousand times with her first instinct always to check and see if he'd left. And that made her angry—not with him, but with herself.

By 7:00 a.m. she was wide awake, watching Tucker sleep and cursing herself. How had she let her heart get involved? This time she couldn't blame it on her father's casually insincere promise or Aiden's choice of a job over her. She couldn't even blame Tucker for having never outgrown a childhood spent moving from place to place. She could only blame herself.

She'd gone into his arms with full foreknowledge of who and what he was, and she'd fallen anyway.

She rolled onto her back, away from Tucker, and said aloud, "I couldn't help myself." She nearly laughed at the absurdity of it, but there was truth to the words. The chemistry between them had been nearly palpable from the very first meeting, but over the past few weeks, and particularly the past few days, she had gotten to know him.

As a man, Tucker was stubborn and opinionated and didn't hesitate to express his opinions. That made him like Cassie, who was one of Alissa's favorite people in the world. But unlike Cassie, Tucker wasn't trying to prove himself to the world. He simply knew his stuff and wanted the job done right. She could respect that. She *did* respect that.

Though she wouldn't admit it under pain of death, part of her had liked the way he'd stepped in and protected her, the way he hadn't backed down when she got in his face. Hell with it. She'd even started to like the whole holding-the-door thing.

Bad sign.

Stomach twisted in miserable knots, she swung to the side of the bed and was mostly relieved when he didn't stir. She wondered whether he was playing possum, then decided she didn't care. If he didn't want to deal with her, then she didn't want to deal with him, either.

On a wistful sigh, she pushed up from the bed and headed for the shower. It was time to get to work. She was halfway to the bathroom, trying not to feel weird about being naked, when the phone rang. She scooped it up on the fly and grabbed a rarely worn robe from her closet. Tucker's dusky eyelashes fluttered and he moved restlessly, closer to awake than asleep.

She held the phone to hear ear as she shrugged into the robe, needing the illusion of armor. "Hello?"

An unfamiliar male voice said, "Good morning. I think we've got something on your footprint."

"Chief Parry?" she asked, utterly confused. "Is that you?" And if so, why call her personally?

"Not Parry," the voice answered, "it's Agent Varitek. We thought—"

A scuffling sound interrupted the deep voice and a

familiar female voice said, "Alissa? Sorry about that. I was going to call you myself, but..." Frustration etched Cassie's normally sharp tone, but she paused and took a breath. "Never mind. Not the important thing right now." Varitek said something in the background, but Alissa didn't catch anything beyond a similar level of frustration. Obviously not a match made in heaven, those two.

Alissa quickly abandoned the idea of a shower, and turned to her closet and clean-laundry pile for clothes. "What have you got? Special-order shoe?"

"It's not the shoe, although you're right that there's no way it would fit Ferguson," Cassie said, excitement sparking in her tone. "It's better than that. We found something in the track itself. Your snow wax picked up some fibers that shouldn't have been in Bear Claw Canyon."

"Bingo!" Alissa held the phone away for a moment to yank the shirt over her head. As she did so, she became acutely aware of Tucker's alert eyes watching her motion, aware of the tension that instantly snapped in the air between them. Their night together had been easy. The day after would be less so, but she wouldn't let that matter right now. They had a kidnapper to catch. She returned the phone to her ear. "What sort of fibers?"

"We're working on it. I figured you'd want to know, though. Piedmont got a hit on Michael Swopes, too. He was in the military and has—get this—explosives experience. Looks like Ferguson may've been a totally separate issue."

"Thanks for calling," Alissa said, unsure how to react to that news. "We'll be there in ten minutes."

She hung up the phone before Cassie could ask what had happened with Tucker. And she would ask, Alissa knew. That was what friends did.

She turned toward Tucker and stared at a spot above his head, so she wouldn't be tempted to notice how sexy he looked all bare-chested and rumpled, with the sheet pooled across his lap. "We're needed at the station. Cassie and the FBI guy have some fibers from the footprint."

Tucker scrubbed a hand across his face, then through his dark hair. "Anything on Ferguson?"

"She didn't say, which means probably not." But they were getting close. She could feel the anticipation, or maybe the nerves hum along her skin. She suppressed a shiver and turned away. "Piedmont tracked down some explosives training in Michael Swopes's past, though, so it sounds like things are finally starting to move. I'll make coffee while you shower, if you want. We don't have much time."

The countdown was running in her head. Actually, two countdowns—one for the amount of time the missing girls had been gone, and one for the amount of time left in her relationship with Tucker. The second countdown had a few more days on it, but not many.

Not enough.

The thought brought a beat of sadness and a louder prickle of irritation. She walked to the kitchen and started the coffee while the aggravation built. Why couldn't he see that they were good together? Why didn't he think about staying? Hell, why didn't he at least offer to do something long-distance? It wasn't ideal, but it wasn't unheard of, either.

Maybe, she thought as she filled a pair of travel mugs, maybe he hadn't suggested it because he'd been living one pattern for so long he didn't know how to change it, didn't even know where to start.

So what if she started? What if she asked him to stay past the couple of weeks he had left? What then?

The phone rang again, distracting her from her thoughts. Figuring it was Cassie again, she answered, "Any news on the fibers?"

There was a pause, then an unfamiliar male voice said, "I'm sorry. This is Chief Whitethorne of the Rock Creek PD. Dispatch gave me this number as a way to reach Tucker McDermott. Is he available?"

Rock Creek. The two words hit her like a gut punch, reminding her that her thoughts of Tucker staying put were nothing more than fantasies. A couple of weeks and he'd be gone.

Unless she put those weeks to good use and convinced him to stay, she thought, a half second before she said, "I'm sorry, Chief Whitethorne, he's in the shower." She'd let Tucker's new boss draw his own conclusions on that. "Can I take a message?"

"Sure. Please let him know that I'll be off duty when he arrives tomorrow, so he should report to Lieutenant Justin Roanoke instead."

Alissa nearly parroted back the word *tomorrow,* but

stopped herself as pain and anger rushed to fill the sudden void in her stomach. "I'll give him the message. Thank you."

She hung up the phone with numb fingers and battled the sudden press of tears, of incredulity. The bastard had moved up his timetable. Worse, he'd known that he was leaving so soon, and hadn't told her before they made love.

It probably wouldn't have made a difference, she admitted to herself. Then again, maybe it would have. He hadn't offered her that choice. And now he was leaving.

She glanced out the front window and saw that, true to their word, her insurance company had dropped off a loaner car for her to drive while they processed the check for her totaled VW.

Hell, she thought, at least she had wheels now. Unfortunately, the prospect didn't improve her mood.

She heard the bathroom door open and close, and then he was standing in her bedroom doorway, looking impossibly sexy with his hair slightly damp and the shadow of a beard on his jaw. Her heart turned in her chest and then died, knowing there was no changing the nature of a man.

So instead of shouting, instead of demanding an explanation, she merely handed him the coffee. "Chief Whitethorne called. He said you're to report to Justin Roanoke tomorrow when you get to your new post."

And she turned and walked away.

Chapter Thirteen

Tucker's first thought was to curse Whitethorne for not leaving a message on his cell phone. It was a shame that he hadn't been the one to tell Alissa, that she'd heard about it from someone else. Not the same as walking out on her, but he would bet it felt damn close, given her history.

He shrugged and said, "I'm sorry. I should have told you last night."

She lifted her chin, not giving him an inch. "Why didn't you?"

"I don't know." He placed the coffee on an end table, wanting his hands free, though not sure quite what to do with them. "I wasn't sure how to handle it. I—" He broke off and scrubbed a hand across his face. "Hell, I don't know."

She shoved her hands in her pockets. "Well, that's helpful. Let's make it simple, then. You're not leaving me tomorrow, because there's nothing to leave. I want you out of here, and I want you out of my life. You're no better than my father or Aiden. In fact, you're worse, because you seem to pride yourself on being honest and keeping people at arm's length, but when it comes right down to it, you're just a coward." She yanked on her parka with short, jerky motions. "I don't need a coward in my life, and I don't need you. Consider our so-called partnership finished a day early, McDermott. I'm headed to the station."

"Wait!" Tucker said quickly. But when she turned and stared at him, he couldn't come up with the right thing to say. Damn it—this was why he stuck to vacation flings. No harm, no foul. But he'd hurt her. He could see it in her eyes. He could feel it in the pressure in his chest, the panic in his gut.

"Well?" she said, her expression not giving an inch.

Unable to find the right words, he said, "You'll need a ride to the station."

Her eyes blanked, as though that was the final straw. But instead of cursing him or laying him bare, she simply shook her head. "Pretty lame, McDermott." Then she turned away and called over her shoulder, "I don't need a ride, I've got a loaner. But that should make you happy. It means you can take your ass to Rock Creek a day early. Don't worry about me, I'll be fine. I'm a big girl. I knew the rules going in."

She slammed the door behind her, leaving Tucker alone. The words *no harm, no foul* chased through his brain. Only, there had been harm.

He'd been harmed. And that was a first.

ANGER PROPELLED ALISSA to the loaner car and down the street, out of Tucker's sight. Then she cracked. She pulled onto a side street and parked in front of a fire hydrant.

And burst into tears.

"Damn it," she said. "Damn him." She folded her arms on the steering wheel and pressed her forehead against them. A headache pounded at her temples, feeding on fatigue, stress and sorrow. Maybe it wasn't fair of her to be so upset—he'd only done what he'd promised all along.

But, damn it, what they had was special. Worth fighting for.

Wasn't it?

In the early-morning quiet, punctuated only by her sniffles, she heard her cell phone ring. She pawed in her pocket for the phone. "Hello?"

"It's Cass. We've identified the fibers!" At a mumble in the background, Cassie's voice dropped a reluctant notch. "Okay, fine. Varitek identified the fibers."

Alissa closed her eyes against the throbbing in her skull. "What are they?"

"Horse hair," Cassie answered. "Any of your suspects involved with horses?" Her voice dropped a satisfied notch. "Because if they are, we've got ourselves a possible connection."

Alissa frowned and forced her mind onto the case, onto the suspects and the scenes. "What did the chief say?"

"That the officers on scene didn't always note the

pets," Cassie said, disgust evident in her voice. "They don't seem to realize we can DNA-type pet hair just as easily as human hair these days. So we were hoping you might remember, since that's your thing. You see a horse anywhere on your travels?"

An image cut through the blurring headache and sliced into her consciousness. "No, but one of the suspects has a really ugly Victorian couch."

She slapped the loaner into drive and hit the accelerator as Cassie barked questions into her ear.

Alissa rattled off the address. "Have backup meet me there. And tell Tucker…" She paused and felt a beat of anger mixed with sadness. "Never mind. Don't tell him a damn thing. I don't need him."

TUCKER CURSED as he drove, hoping the anger would heal the part inside him that felt as if it had come unhinged when he'd seen the pain in Alissa's eyes. Pain he'd put there by being selfish. That was it—he wasn't a coward as she'd called him, he was selfish. He'd wanted her, and on some level he'd known she wouldn't have spent the night with him knowing it was nearly his last in Bear Claw.

It had been a lie of omission, and he'd hurt a good woman. Hell, he'd hurt himself, and he hadn't expected that. Always before he had been the one to walk away, the one to feel less pain than his partner. Frankly, he'd been the one to feel nothing beyond the itchy restlessness that told him it was time to move on, time to see new sights, meet new people.

Where was that restlessness now? He'd been nearly overwhelmed by it in the past few months, the sort of maddening heat that drove him from place to place. That was why he'd put in for the transfer to Rock Creek a week or so after Alissa and her friends had taken over Fitz's place at the BCCPD.

A connection jabbed at his brain, but he didn't want to make it, didn't want to see the logic of something he couldn't believe in. Alissa's arrival had nothing to do with the restlessness. She couldn't. He cursed, and floored the accelerator until the SUV fishtailed into the BCCPD parking lot. He didn't see Alissa's car, but he'd only caught a glimpse of the unfamiliar vehicle as she'd sped off.

He took the steps two at a time, trying to think of what he could say to make this right, whether it was possible to ever make it right. He opened the door and met Cassie coming the other way, eyes alight with excitement. When she saw him, those eyes immediately darkened. "What the hell did you do to Alissa? When I talked to her on the phone she'd been *crying*. Alissa never cries!"

He didn't bother to contradict her, didn't bother to defend himself because his brain locked on a single word. "On the phone? Why were you talking on the phone? She's here, isn't she?"

Cassie shook her head, and Tucker became aware of the FBI agent at her back and the fact that they were both wearing outdoor clothes and an air of hurry. They were headed out.

"She's on the road," Cassie answered, confirming the

ice-cold fear that suddenly crystallized in his gut. "She's on her way to Bradford Croft's place. His mother has a horsehair sofa."

Tucker was running to his vehicle before she even finished her sentence, with one thought pounding in his brain.

He had to get to her before Croft did.

Alissa pulled into the Walshes' driveway, knowing that Lizzie and her family were still at the hospital. Over the churn in her stomach, she blessed the nondescript loaner, which didn't look anything like a cop car and wouldn't spook the neighbors.

More specifically, it wouldn't spook Bernard Croft, whose mother owned a ratty horsehair sofa. Some might call it a tenuous link, but it was what she had, what she would run with. True, Croft had seemingly solid alibis for two of the relevant time periods, but the alibis could be faked, or the time periods could be slightly off. Stranger things had happened.

Alissa took a breath and clicked off her seat belt. She should wait for backup. It was protocol. But her instincts prickled a warning. Something didn't feel right.

She scanned the scene, comparing mental snapshots to her impressions from previous visits. Something was different about the Croft house, but what? She wasn't sure, but her gut hummed with an inexplicable urgency that told her she needed to move now, not wait for backup. Somehow, somewhere the missing girls needed her to move this very instant.

Her cell phone rang, jolting her. She flipped it open. "Hello?"

She expected it to be Cassie with more information, or with an ETA on the others. Instead Tucker's voice snapped, "Alissa? Stay put. I'm on my way."

Her body washed cold and then hot with anger. Her throat tightened, but she refused to waste any more tears on him. At least not right now. She had a job to do.

She gritted her teeth and cursed the twist of grief when his voice came through the phone. "Alissa? Are you there?"

She had said her goodbye at the house, unplanned though it had been. Part of her had hoped he'd pack up and go. It would have made things easier. But because he hadn't, because his voice demanded an answer, she said, "I'm here. I'll wait."

And then she did what she swore she'd never do. She broke protocol because of a gut feeling. She tossed the phone on the passenger seat of the loaner car and closed the door with a decisive thump.

Then she set off across Lizzie's yard, toward the Croft house. She circled the building on foot, hoping for a clue, but the shades were drawn over all the windows except the one beside the front door.

Hearing nothing, seeing nothing, and driven by a pounding sense of urgency, Alissa framed her face with her hands and peeked through. She gasped and reeled back before training kicked in and sent her to the door. She didn't bother knocking, didn't identify herself. She didn't need to, based on what she'd just seen.

Esmerelda Croft lay on the starchy maroon sofa in the front room, hands folded across her small breasts, throat slashed from ear to ear.

The doorknob twisted easily in her hand, both a relief and a concern. She was glad not to waste the energy on breaking down the door, but worried that Croft had left it open, as though he didn't care when his mother was found.

As though his plans had already moved beyond her.

Gun in hand, Alissa opened the door and waited, listening. Hearing nothing, she eased inside the front room. Her heart hammered in her ears, and adrenaline surged through her, leaving her legs tingling to run, her chest aching to scream.

Instead, she forced herself to breathe normally and walked to the sofa. She scanned the scene and wished she had her camera. But there would be time for the full processing later. Right now, she needed to know where Croft had gone. Where he was keeping Maria and Holly.

Whether or not they were alive.

Mastering her speeding heart by force of will, Alissa crossed to the sofa and stood looking down, senses widened to encompass the crime scene.

Blood pooled beneath the sofa, dark where it had seeped into the waxed wood floor and soaked the corner of a worn department-store carpet. The slice across Esmerelda's throat still leaked wetly, and when Alissa let her free hand hover over the woman's skin, she could feel a faint trickle of warmth.

Bradford's mother hadn't been dead long.

Even more chilling, the killer had placed the handle

of a bloodstained carving knife in her hands where they folded across her chest, like another, saner son might have placed a rose.

Alissa swallowed against the mad logic of it, then turned away from the body. Time was passing. The others would be here soon. Protocol demanded that she return to her vehicle, call in the murder and wait for backup.

Instead she stepped further into the house, both hands on her weapon. There was something else here at the scene. She could feel it.

A flash of motion at the corner of her eye sent her heart into her throat. "Surprise!" Bradford Croft lunged at her from behind a nearby door, slamming into her and driving her to her knees.

Alissa screamed, dropped and rolled, trying to keep moving in the narrow hallway while she brought her weapon to bear.

Croft loomed over her, mouth stretched wide in a half-mad rictus of excitement and blood lust. His hazel eyes were glazed, the pupils dilated, making her wonder whether he was hopped up on something, or had simply gone over to a world of his own making.

Her gut told her the latter, which made him that much more dangerous.

He kicked at her, stomping down with large lace-up boots. She rolled out of the way and struggled to her feet as the mental image of his wide-ribbed boot tread lined up with the cast she'd lifted from the canyon.

Though she hadn't needed the additional proof, her

analyst's brain filed the information even as her cop's training had her lifting her weapon. "Stand down, Croft. Nobody else needs to get hurt."

Dead or alive didn't apply in this case—she needed to take him alive.

His mad grin split wider. "You've got that right. You need me to tell you where the girls are." He closed lightning fast, slamming into her and pinning her against the wall. She fired, but the bullet spent itself in the fabric-covered wall, which spurted a puff of chalky white drywall.

Alissa's lungs squeezed tight against his weight, and pain slammed through her as bone ground against bone. She screamed, but the sound came out paper-thin, and he chuckled when she kicked out and connected only with air.

He drove his elbow into her gut, doubling her over and forcing the last oxygen out of her body. She retched and gasped, head spinning, and felt the gun plucked from her grasp.

"You won't be needing this where you're going."

Help me! she shouted in her brain. From her collapsed position she could see a corner of the sofa and part of the blood pool. *Where the hell are you? I need you!*

She meant her police backup in general, but her mind fixed on Tucker's image, on Tucker's protection.

Her lungs unkinked enough to let a thin trickle of air through and she sucked in a breath, enough to clear some of the dizziness. She croaked, "It's over, Croft.

My backup is outside. They'll never let you through. Give up now, tell me where the girls are, and things will go easier on you."

"There's an accident on Main Street," he said conversationally. "Your backup's been delayed. But no worries. I'll be happy to tell you where the girls are. Better yet, why don't I show you?"

She heard a click and snap, and felt the quick tightness of a zip tie around her wrists. She screamed and thrashed, but he quickly linked her ankles, as well, then punched her in the side of the head. He scooped up her fallen weapon, lifted her limp, dazed body in his arms and said, "It's not far. But it's very well hidden, so don't worry about us being interrupted."

The finality of it screamed through Alissa as he slung her over his shoulder and carried her through the house and out the back door, where a neatly trimmed pine hedge hid the yard from view.

He dumped her roughly into the back seat of an older Jeep and slammed the door, catching her bound feet between the seat and the door. Alissa bowed back against the pain, but used it to clear her head. Sort of.

She strained to detect sirens in the distance, but heard only silence, which made no sense. He had mentioned an accident, but how had he known? Had he orchestrated it himself? But if so, how had he been in two places at once?

Croft fired the engine and sent the Jeep out the long driveway and through the housing development. They didn't pass any BCCPD vehicles.

Fear ached through Alissa like pain. A traitorous, unprofessional tear broke free and streamed down her cheek.

Tucker, where the hell are you?

TUCKER PULLED STRAIGHT into Croft's driveway, followed a second later by at least half the task force. He glanced over at Alissa's borrowed car in the next driveway and didn't even bother to curse when he saw that it was empty. He'd already figured she'd gone in alone.

She might preach protocol, but when the chips were down, she acted like any good cop. She did what was necessary and bore the consequences.

If he was lucky, the only consequences she'd have to bear would be his hands around her pretty little neck. Shaking her for worrying him. Hugging her for being alive.

She'd damn well better be alive.

Tucker swung down from the SUV, his brain jammed with images. Alissa at the bar that first night, dancing with sensual abandon. Standing in front of the task force, trying to pretend it didn't matter that the BCCPD wished her gone. Getting in his face over a thousand tiny things. Sleeping beside him in the wee hours of that morning. Glaring at him with her heart in her eyes after Whitethorne's call.

And last and most terrifying, he imagined her caught by Croft, taken somewhere, too late for him to follow.

The words *too damn late* chased him up the walk to Croft's house, with most of the BCCPD police force at his back. He saw a set of fresh tire tracks curving from the back of the house to the plowed and salted driveway, and cursed his quick suspicion.

The front door yielded beneath his fingertips, and he turned back to get Chief Parry's go-ahead, but the chief wasn't there.

And why did that detail give him the faintest sense of wrongness?

He banished the thought, gestured Mendoza and Piedmont to flank him and stepped inside the Croft residence, weapon at the ready.

The smell hit him first, cloying and dark in the overheated house, a mix of blood and the body fluids that follow violent death. He swallowed, but couldn't move the hard ball of dread sitting on his chest. "Well, hell. He killed his mother."

"Never mind that now," Mendoza said. "Where's Wyatt?"

"Gone," Tucker said flatly, not needing a search to confirm what his gut and heart already knew. "The bastard took her."

He sent the others through the house while Cassie and Varitek took control of the murder scene. "Find me anything you can," he told them. "There's got to be a hint where he's gone. Assume he's taken her to wherever he's stashed the girls. And now that he's progressed to murder..." Tucker couldn't finish the sentence, but he saw the knowledge in Cassie's eyes.

Now the girls' lives were measured in minutes or hours, not days. Alissa's, too.

The last thought nearly closed Tucker's throat in

panic. How had he let this happen? He was supposed to be protecting her. How had he let his own agenda get in the way of that?

A touch at his shoulder startled him, as did the compassion in Piedmont's eyes. "She knew the risks, and she can take care of herself. She's a cop."

Tucker shook him off. "She's my cop. My responsibility. I—" *love her*, he almost said. The words jammed in his throat, nearly paralyzing him with the truth of it.

Impossible, he thought. He couldn't love her. It wasn't in his makeup. He was the guy who never felt enough when it mattered.

"I know." Piedmont nodded, eyes dark with sympathy. "So go get her."

"I don't even know where to start." Frustration built in Tucker's chest, in his gut. "Don't you get it? We've been looking for this guy for nearly a month now, and we don't know where he takes them. None of it makes any sense!" He wanted to kick something, punch something, beat the truth out of the man who had left probably only moments ahead of their arrival.

He wanted to rage, he wanted to shout, he wanted to have Alissa in his arms, wanted to tell her he was sorry for fighting what was between them.

Hell, he wanted to beg her to let him stay.

Stunned by the realization, he turned away from Piedmont, away from the body and the cops who moved from room to room, looking for something that could send them to the rescue. Something. Anything.

The futility of it hollowed his chest. He wanted to stay with her. He wanted to stay in Bear Claw Creek, or wherever she wanted to be. It had never been about the places, he realized. He hadn't been seeking new places. He'd been in search of his partner. His anchor.

And now that he'd found her, he might already have lost her.

He cursed, holstered his weapon and scrubbed both hands across his face, trying to will the others to find something, trying to will Croft to make a mistake, to will Alissa to take action.

If she was still able to.

Refusing to consider the other alternative, he thought as hard as he could, *Come on, Alissa. I need some help here.* As he did so, he realized it was the first time he'd consciously asked for something from a woman, something beyond quick physical release or a surface good time.

Incredibly, a nearby patrolman's radio squawked with incoming news of an accident near Bear Claw Canyon. Motorists had phoned in news of a Jeep abandoned in a ditch. The tags matched a vehicle registered to Bradford Croft.

Angry adrenaline spiked through Tucker's body and he fisted his hands at his sides, wishing he had them wrapped around Croft's neck. "Gotcha, you bastard!"

Thanks to Alissa, they had their break. He had to believe the accident was Alissa's doing, had to believe she was still alive, still fighting.

The alternative was too terrible to consider.

"She'd better be alive," he said aloud, not caring who heard him. "I have to tell her I love her."

Chapter Fourteen

In the pine woods just east of Bear Claw Canyon, Alissa stumbled and scuffed her feet, part strategy and part necessity. The snow dragged her down just as surely as Croft hauled her forward toward his hideout.

The lack of tracks worried her. Nobody had come this way in days, since before the last big snowfall, which had happened the night of Lizzie's return.

"Hurry up." Croft yanked at the rope he'd tied to the double-thick zip that was fastened around her wrists, causing the plastic to bite into her chilled skin. "You think that stunt with the Jeep is going to help you? Think again. By the time your pathetic cop friends have found it, you'll already be gone." He patted the front pocket of his puffy tan parka, where he'd tucked her weapon. "If you're lucky, I'll do you quickly."

"Same goes for you," she said through chattering teeth. After she'd lurched into the front seat and yanked the emergency brake, causing them to spin out and flip into a ditch, he'd hauled her from the vehicle, yanked out a knife that was second cousin to the one he'd left in his mother's hands, and cut her parka off her. Then he'd pulled off her gloves and boots, leaving her cold and unprotected. Refusing to be cowed, she lifted her chin to say, "And if you're not lucky, I'll let McDermott have you first."

Even saying his name gave her a burst of renewed energy, of hope. Surely he was coming for her.

Why would you think that? her insecurities asked. *You sent him away, told him you never wanted to see him again. That's what he was waiting for. Permission to leave.*

The last thought gave her pause because it rang of truth.

"Forget that," she spat as her heart broke in her chest. "I don't need backup. I can handle you myself."

"No, you can't." he said. "We're almost there, and your hands have got to be feeling numb by now. What are you going to do?" He stopped and walked back to her, rope held loosely in one hand. He reached into his pocket and withdrew her gun. "You going to wrestle me for this?" He gestured to his other pocket, where he'd tucked the knife after he cut the zip ties binding her ankles, so she could walk. "You going to grab the knife and cut yourself loose?" He stepped even closer, his mad eyes taunting her, mocking her. "What are you going to do, Officer Wyatt? How are you going to save yourself?"

She screeched and lunged at him, swinging her bound hands at his head, hoping to bludgeon him to the ground. Her near-frozen feet folded beneath her and she fell to her knees in the snow, which was quickly spotted red from the cuts on her wrists. The world spun, warning her that she had probably hit her head during the wreck, though she remembered little of it.

"Damn it." Tears pressed at her eyes, hot in contrast to the numbing cool that spread through her body. "Damn you. Why are you doing this?"

He chuckled, shoved the gun in his parka and used the rope to haul her onto the numb blocks of ice that had once been her feet. "Because I can. Because it's fun. Because it's all part of the grand plan." He stilled for a moment, head cocked to one side as though he was listening to an inner voice. "I never had the guts before to stand up to my mother. It was always, 'Bradford do this,' and 'Bradford do that.' Or 'Bradford, you're no damn good. No wonder your father ran off.'"

An inner chill chased through Alissa at the parallel, adding to the cold numbness. She licked her lips and braced her legs when they wanted to wobble. "My father took off, too. Trust me, it wasn't your fault. It was his."

But the brave words rang ever so slightly false, as though she didn't really believe it, even after all these years.

Croft snorted as if he, too, heard the insecurity. "It doesn't matter anymore. I'm the collector. I've gathered a few friends who understand me. People who don't judge me the way my parents did, the way you're judging me right now."

"I'm not—" Alissa began, but Croft was done talking. He turned away and yanked her in his wake, nearly dragging her off her feet before she could force herself to stumble after him. But as she staggered through the drifts and tried not to worry that Croft clearly didn't care about leaving a trail for the others to follow, she kept thinking, *What friends?*

Was he talking about the kidnapped girls? Had his delusional brain redefined the hostages as his friends? Or was he talking about someone else?

A connection tweaked at her, then was gone as he dragged her into a clearing beneath a nondescript stand of trees. A shallow dip in the snow showed where the area had been plowed a few storms ago, and a similar depression snaked away from the clearing, evidence of a road or track leading out through the state forest.

It took a moment for her snow-blinded eyes to adjust to the dimness beneath the trees, but once her vision cleared, she saw three prefab sheds, partially buried beneath layers of snow. Though she had half expected to see the sheds, the reality of them shook her. Scared her. Weakened her already weak limbs.

"In you go!" Croft dragged her to the first of the sheds, shot a heavy metal slide bolt on the outside and yanked the door open. The midday winter sun filtered through the trees overhead and fell on the motionless, thinly clad body of a dark-haired girl whose skin carried the pale cast of death. Without bothering to untie the rope fastened to her wrist bonds, he shoved Alissa inside.

She screamed as her legs finally gave out, sending her crashing to the floor beside the girl's body. She hit hard and nearly blacked out from the impact of her head against the solid plywood floor.

"Stay there," he said, as if she was capable of going

anywhere. "I'll go get the other one. It's easier to light just the one fire."

He slammed the door and shot the bolt, leaving Alissa alone. For the moment.

"Oh, God. Help me. Please help me." Alissa heard the whispered mantra coming from her own lips, and was unsurprised when it morphed to a plaintive, "Hurry up, Tucker. I need you. You've got to get me out of here. Please, hurry."

She held his image, untamed and faintly distrustful, in her mind's eye and went to work on the zip ties. Her wrists were sticky with blood, but the wetness helped. She managed to pull one hand partway through, but it stuck at the wide part just before her thumb joint. "Come on. Come on! He's going to be back here any second."

It wouldn't take long for Croft to collect "the other one." She didn't even want to think about his mention of fire. It made too much insidious sense. He would kill her and set the shed ablaze. The smoke would bring the authorities, but hadn't that been his attention all along?

Attract attention. Keep the cops guessing.

What she didn't understand was *why*. He'd mentioned a grand plan. His? Someone else's? What the hell was going on here?

But that didn't matter now. What mattered was getting out. Getting back to Tucker. Apologizing to him for the way she'd behaved that morning. She'd overreacted—she'd admit it now. What was the difference between him leaving in a day or a week? Nothing. Her anger had been an excuse to push him away before he left on his own. A way to protect herself from heart-break by making it her idea.

Only, it hadn't protected her one bit. She'd simply added rage to the heartache. And for what? Something that seemed so silly and small to her at that moment. Her ego.

But what was ego in the face of death? In the face of love?

There. She'd admitted it. She loved Tucker. As much as she'd tried to keep it from happening, as much as she'd tried to protect herself, she'd gone and fallen in love with him.

And she damn sure wasn't giving up on him. She was going to fight for him, make him see that he didn't need to keep moving. And if he did...she'd just move right along with him, she decided then and there. It wouldn't be her first choice, but it would have to do.

Her father hadn't loved her mother enough to make the changes that were needed, and maybe that lack went both ways. There was no way she was letting what was between her and Tucker suffer the same fate. Not if she had anything to say about it.

Unfortunately, she might not.

Footsteps crunched in the snow just as Alissa ripped her hand free. Pain sang up her arm, but she didn't focus on it, couldn't let it slow her down.

Instead, she dragged herself up to her knees and balanced there with the rope knotted in her cold-numbed fingers like a garrote.

She wasn't going down without a fight.

"THERE!" TUCKER SLAMMED on the brakes, and his SUV skidded to a stop ncar the wreck. A Jeep lay on its roof some fifteen feet off the road. A dark shape lay nearby, a motionless scrap of a familiar color.

Alissa's parka.

Tucker's blood ran cold until he realized that the coat was empty, lying beside her gloves and boots. The bastard had hobbled her with the cold. He looked past the jacket and saw two sets of tracks. A smile touched his lips. "Good girl."

She had made sure she'd left her own tracks so it would be obvious that it wasn't just Croft climbing into the forest. But where were they going? What was up there?

Nothing, he thought, nothing but a closed-down fire-access path and a few clearings.

But maybe that was enough.

He hit the gas and drove up the road another quarter mile, then braked at a cut-through in the guardrail. "Sonofagun."

The supposedly closed fire-access road had a new chain and padlock on the pipe gate, and plow marks less than a week old. Tucker dropped his SUV into four-wheel drive, backed up thirty feet crosswise along the road as four BCCPD vehicles came into sight, and hit the gas. The SUV clung to the road, accelerated across the snow and hit the gate with a crunch. The vehicle shuddered, then it broke through and climbed up and over the crumpled gate, slithering in the snow beyond.

Tucker fought the wheel and babied the gas just

enough to keep going forward and semistraight, but didn't let up when the tires spun. He didn't have time for finesse. He had to get to Alissa.

He gunned it up the fire-access road, through thick stands of snow-covered pines that slapped at the windshield and obscured his vision. He broke through and slowed up a moment to get his bearings. Then he saw smoke rising up ahead, too much and too dirty to be a campfire. He cursed and hit the gas.

If he was too late to save Alissa, Bradford Croft was going to die.

ALISSA HELD herself still, barely daring to breathe as the footsteps outside the little shed paused and she heard…voices?

One voice she might have dismissed as Croft's madness talking to itself, but she was certain she heard a second man. She strained to pick out details of the conversation, but could only manage to distinguish a word here or there. When the voices paused, she inhaled and steeled herself to fight two men, not one.

Her indrawn breath contained the smell of smoke. Her heart hammered in her chest, feeling oddly warm and alive in comparison to the rest of her body. Croft had already lit at least one of the other sheds.

The clock was ticking.

A foreign sound startled her from behind, a rustling hiss of motion. She turned cautiously, most of her attention focused on the men she could hear outside, but wary hope sparked in her soul. "Tucker?" she whispered. "Is that you?"

"No," a weak thread of a voice replied, "my name's Maria."

Alissa turned fully at that, a cop's excitement battering away some of the woman's weakness inside her. "You're alive!" She kept her voice at the threshold of hearing, but couldn't hide the joy. "Is Holly okay, too?"

"She was last night," Maria answered through quivering, blue-tinged lips. "We talk, or bang sometimes when our voices give out." A pause. "She didn't answer this morning, though."

And none of it would mean a damn thing, Alissa knew, if she didn't take out Croft and his associate then and there. She tightened her grip on the pitiful length of rope and faced the door. "Stay down and let me handle this. I'm a cop."

Excitement laced the girl's next whisper. "Is this a rescue? Are there others?"

Alissa swallowed, realizing that it was quiet outside the shed, that the men must have turned their attention to the grisly work at hand. "I sure as hell hope so."

Then the slide bolt rattled and the door flung open, and there wasn't time for hope anymore. There was only time to fight.

Or die.

Alissa lunged forward and caught Croft at the knees. He had Holly's limp body slung over his shoulder, and the weight overbalanced him. He fell back with a shout. Holly's limp, lightly clothed form tumbled into a snowdrift.

Alissa flung herself onto Croft's prone body, barely conscious of the heat, light and noise coming from the nearby sheds, which were ablaze with orange flames. She stretched the rope across his windpipe, with a hand on each side and most of her weight bearing down, but the soft snow yielded beneath them, cushioning the attack. She looked around wildly but didn't see the other man, the one Croft had been talking to.

Big mistake. Croft had been waiting for the break in her attention. He scissored his legs up in an unexpectedly dextrous move, grabbed her by the waist and yanked her aside.

Alissa howled and let go of the useless rope. She thrashed wildly in the snow, trying to escape the crushing grip of Croft's thighs. She scrabbled for his coat pockets for a weapon. Knife or gun, she wasn't picky.

He got a grip on her hair and yanked hard. Pain sizzled through her skull and tears filmed her eyes. She screamed and writhed, hating that his superior strength and leverage countered all her trained fighting moves.

Cold wetness surrounded her, numbing and slowing her actions, making everything a little too slippery, which was both a good and bad thing. Good because she was able to wrench free from Croft's leg hold. Bad because he rolled away from her, still in possession of both weapons.

He rose to his knees, fumbling at his right pocket, eyes hot with anger and excitement. "You want to do it this way? That wasn't in the plan, but it's fine by me. You'll all be dead either way." He yanked out Alissa's weapon, checked it, and leveled it at her. "Say your goodbyes."

Near-frozen with panic and cold, Alissa lurched to the side just as a blur flung itself out of the shed and plowed into Croft, foiling his aim. The first shot cracked on the air and went wild, spending itself in one of the burning sheds. He cursed and stood, shaking off Maria's weak attack. He turned cold, dead eyes on the girl and aimed the muzzle of his weapon between her eyes. "Okay, then. You first."

As his finger tightened on the trigger, Alissa launched herself forward. She heard the report of the weapon, close, too close, felt the incongruous heat of muzzle flash, and hit the snow with Maria's body beneath her. She didn't feel pain, didn't feel much of anything beyond numb weariness. She grabbed at Croft's legs, trying to bring him down, but had no leverage, no power.

She rolled over and looked up, directly into the fathomless dark of a muzzle bore. She saw his finger tighten fractionally, saw her own death in his eyes.

TUCKER DROVE THE SUV into the clearing like a madman on a mission, breaking through drifts and ruts and never letting up on the gas. He'd left the other cops lagging behind, driven by the gut-level certainty that Alissa was in grave danger, if she wasn't gone already.

Save her, save her, save her! The litany beat in his brain, telling him what he had only recently realized on his own. He needed her. He loved her.

He passed the first burning structure—sure enough,

it was one of those prefab sheds—and cut the wheel to send the SUV skidding past the second.

And he saw them. His blood iced, freezing with equal parts fear and rage, then bursting through his body in a hot wash of blood lust and revenge.

Bradford Croft stood over three prone figures that Tucker quickly identified as Alissa and the two missing girls.

None of the women were moving.

"No!" Tucker slammed on the brakes, slapped the SUV's transmission into park and erupted from the vehicle, ready to do battle, to do murder. "You *bastard!*"

Knowing he couldn't pull his weapon and bring down Croft quickly enough, Tucker howled as he lunged at the man, hoping to distract him, to delay him.

Sure enough, Croft turned to focus on the new threat, taking his attention off the women for just long enough. Tucker crashed into the bastard, catching him at the waist and sending the gun flying. The men landed in a tangle in the cold snow and rolled, punching and grunting and swearing.

Croft jammed an elbow into Tucker's jaw hard enough to send his head ringing. A lucky chop sent Tucker's gun spinning away, and he retaliated with a pair of gut punches that would have felled an ordinary man. But Croft, fueled by desperation and madness, merely grunted and grabbed for his left coat pocket.

"Tucker!" Alissa screamed. "Watch out, he's got a knife!"

She was alive! Her welcome, blessed voice distracted him with the knowledge, diverting his attention a second too long.

Croft yanked a ten-inch blade from his parka and brandished it with a cruel, excited smile. "I've got a knife, all right, and I'm going to cut you with it. You, then the girls. Who should go first? The cop, I think. I'm bored with the others."

Out of time, out of options, Tucker lunged with a roar and caught Croft around the midsection. He grabbed the bastard's knife hand in a firm grip, and the men went reeling across the boot-churned snow. Tucker's feet slipped, and he stumbled forward, pushing Croft ahead of him as they struggled for control of the knife.

Attention wholly focused on his enemy and on the knife, Tucker only peripherally heard Alissa's anguished scream of, "Tuck-errrr!"

Then he and Croft fell together into the burning wreckage of the second shed. Flaming wood collapsed beneath them with a crash and shower of burning sparks, and Tucker's lungs seized on themselves, fighting the choking smoke and sulfur burn. Croft screeched and writhed, nearly reversing their positions. But Tucker was bigger and stronger. He jammed an elbow into Croft's gut and evaded a wild swing of the knife. He grabbed Croft's wrist and twisted until the knife fell free, within reach. He grabbed the weapon and hauled Croft away from the shed, which roared furnace-hot.

Behind him, he heard approaching shouts and footsteps as the BCCPD reinforcements arrived. He looked from the mad blood lust in Croft's eyes to the knife and back to Croft, and thought about what the bastard had tried to do to Alissa. Thought about what he would have done if Tucker had arrived a moment later. Thought about shoving the knife home and pushing Croft further into the flames.

The wildness surged within him, but was stemmed only by two quiet words. "Tucker, don't."

And then she was at his side, touching his arm and gently taking the knife away. "I'm okay. The girls are okay. You've got him." Her eyes darkened. "And we need him for information. There's more to this case than we thought. I think there's a second man."

"You'll get nothing from me!" Croft stepped back toward the fire. "You stupid cops don't understand anything. Not one thing, and I'm not going to be the one to explain it!" Lightning quick, he darted off to the side of the burning shed, reached down and scooped up one of the fallen weapons.

"Alissa!" Tucker grabbed her and shielded her with his body, putting himself between her and the gun, bracing for the burn of impact.

The weapon discharged with a crack that was echoed in the roar of flame, but Tucker felt no thud of impact, no burn of entry. Instead, Croft jerked like a stringless marionette and spun in a slow, bloody circle with half his head gone. He reeled one step, then another, and then collapsed through the side wall of the burning structure.

The shed gave with a groan and a crash, and the roof collapsed onto Croft's motionless form.

And he was gone.

Tucker knew he couldn't save Croft from his own destruction. So he tightened his arms around Alissa and buried his face in her hair. She was shivering, shaking, quaking against him, likely as much from cold as from shock.

"McDermott, Wyatt, are you two okay?" a deep, familiar voice asked.

Tucker looked up to find Chief Parry opposite him, flanked by almost the entire task force. His tired brain tried to wonder how the chief had gotten there when he hadn't been in any of the cars, but he couldn't deal with such things right then. Not with the warmth of burning wood at his back and the too-cool feel of the woman in his arms.

"I'm taking her in to warm up," Tucker announced. Then, not caring what sort of message he was sending, he scooped her up into his arms and held her socked feet out of the snow. "She'll report in later, after you guys have taken care of the girls and mopped up this garbage." He flicked a hand at the now-guttering fires and Croft's body, which was being dragged from the smoldering mess.

Without waiting for a by-your-leave from his chief—heck, Parry wasn't even his chief anymore, he was technically unemployed if he didn't show up in Rock Creek the following day—Tucker turned away.

He wanted to get her alone. He had a few things he needed to say to her.

A few things he needed to hear in return.

ALISSA LET HER HEAD FALL BACK against Tucker's chest, wishing it was really over. But it wasn't. Not by a long

shot. She touched his arm. "Wait. This is important."
When he'd turned back to the others, she took a deep
breath and said, "There was another man. I heard them
talking. This was a team job. We've got to find the other
guy."

A murmur of surprise ran through the assembled
members of the BCCPD task force. Maya stepped
forward, eyes worried. "Are you sure?"

"Of course I'm sure," Alissa snapped. "I'm not delusional. I'm perfectly fine." But her teeth chattered as
she said it.

Cassie spoke slowly, as though she were choosing
her words with great care. "I'm sorry, 'Lissa. There
weren't any tire tracks other than McDermott's, no
vehicle, and no evidence of foot traffic other than you
and Croft hiking in from the wreck site."

"But he was here, I'm sure of it." Alissa gritted her
teeth against the racking shivers, which seemed to be
growing worse rather than better as Tucker's warmth
seeped into her bones. "Croft talked about 'our plan.'
Plural. There was someone else in on this. I swear it."

Chief Parry nodded, though his eyes said he didn't
buy it for a second. "We'll look for evidence of a second
kidnapper, you can be sure of that." Humor lighted in
his tired-looking eyes. "Don't forget, we have one of the
best crime scene units in the state."

She could see from his expression that she would
have to live with that. So she nodded. "Thanks, Chief."

This time she didn't protest when Tucker turned
away. She nodded to acknowledge Cassie's and Maya's

waves, knowing they would want to hear the full story later. But between now and then, she had one last battle to win or lose. One last opponent.

Tucker.

He loaded her into his SUV, stripped off her soaking wet socks and sweater, and bundled her into his leather jacket, all without speaking. Then he shut the door and worked his way around to the driver's side. He slapped the still-running vehicle into Drive, maneuvered it through the crush of BCCPD vehicles in the smallish clearing and sent his vehicle along the churned-up track.

She shifted to face him, and her stomach dropped at the sight of his tense profile and the bunched muscle beside his jaw. He looked furious. She reached out to touch him. "Tucker, I—"

He lifted a hand in warning. "Not now. Give me a minute."

Startled by his rough, strained tone, Alissa shrank back into her seat until irritation sent her forward again. "Hey, there's no call for you to be—"

He spun the SUV into a clearing and slammed on the parking brake. Then he reached over and dragged her out of the passenger seat, wet clothes and all, and pulled her onto his lap.

She squeaked and batted at his hands. "Tucker! What—"

"Hush." He folded her into his arms and squeezed so tight she could barely breathe. "Just let me hold you. I thought I'd lost you. I thought I was too late."

Tears backed up in her throat at the ragged grief in

his voice, and she twisted around so she could touch a hand to his face. She was still trembling, she thought, even though the heater was going full blast and she didn't feel nearly as cold anymore.

No, she realized. She wasn't the one trembling. He was.

Her heart cracked, letting the pain in, letting the hope in. She reached up and touched her lips to his. "I'm okay. You got there in time."

The kiss started out gentle, soothing, a way of saying *I'm here, I'm fine,* but it soon spiraled into something hot and greedy and needy. His tongue swept into her mouth, possessing, dominating, branding his taste onto her every molecule.

She moaned and fisted her hands in his hair, in his damp shirt, and he tore his mouth away from hers to place a fervent line of kisses along her jaw, her neck, her brow, anyplace he could reach without letting go of her.

The passion nearly undid her, and her tears broke free when he said, "I'm sorry about all of it. Sorry for my stupid rules and for not telling you about Rock Creek. I'm sorry for not figuring out sooner that all this time, I haven't been itching to leave Bear Claw, I've been itching to have you, to be with you. To love you." He paused and she felt a huge shudder wrack his body. But when his eyes met hers, they were clear and free of conflict for the first time since she'd met him. "I do love you, you know. I love you and I want to stay here with you, if you'll have me."

Alissa's heart contracted and then exploded in a million glittering shards of joy. "Yes, absolutely! I'll have you. I want you to stay. Or I'll go with you, whatever you want. I was going to tell you that, only you beat me to it, you rat!"

He shuddered again, and the tension drained from him in an instant. He grinned, a ghost of that cocky, wild-man's expression that had drawn her across a crowded dance floor. "Tell me what?"

"That I love you!" she said, nearly shouting the words with joy at being able to set them free and have them returned to her. "I love you, Tucker McDermott. And I'm not going to let you go."

"I'm not going anywhere," he vowed, touching his lips to her cheek. "I'm staying right here with you."

She turned her lips to his and poured herself into a heated kiss. A faint hiss of ice against glass told her that the capricious Colorado winter was dumping yet more snow on them. She let her eyelids flutter shut as Tucker's hands drifted beneath the warm, man-smelling leather jacket and shaped her body, which definitely wasn't feeling the cold anymore.

In a corner of her cop's mind, she worried about the other man she had heard talking to Croft. She hadn't imagined him. She was sure of it. The evidence might not back her up, but she had learned a little bit about trusting her gut, and her instincts told her there was another kidnapper out there, one smart enough to hide his tracks. Would he strike again in Bear Claw City? Only time would tell, and she vowed to keep a sharp eye out for the possibility.

But for the first time in her life, she wouldn't be

going it alone. She would have a partner, a wingman, a lover.

Someone she could trust not to leave.

On that thought, she opened her eyes and focused on the snowy pines beyond the gently fogging glass. When their kiss paused, she pulled away a fraction of an inch and said, "So where's home going to be? Bear Claw? Rock Creek? Somewhere else?"

He shook his head and said, "Doesn't matter where. You're my home."

Then he kissed her again, and there was no more thought of words.

There was only love.

* * * * *

*Be sure to pick up Jessica Andersen's next
heart-stopping romantic suspense when*
Bear Claw Creek Crime Lab *continues with*
*AT CLOSE RANGE,
coming in April 2006!*

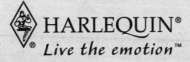